DELTA PEARLS

DELTA PEARLS

JUDITH BADER JONES

SWEETGUM PRESS

WARRENSBURG, MISSOURI

Published by Sweetgum Press,
Warrensburg, Missouri
Printed on acid-free paper

Some pieces in this book appeared, in slightly different form, in the
following publications: "Across the River" and "The Petrified Man
and My New York Grandmother" in *Art Times*; "My Delta Pearls"
in *Buffalo Spree*; "Plastic Curtains" in *Chocolate for a Teen's Spirit*;
"Missouri Bootheel Cold" in the *Kansas City Star*; "Mornings and
Mama" in *Kansas City Star Magazine*; "Billie Jean," "They Laid
Their Cards on the Table," and "Between the Lines" in *Potpourri*;
"Red Flannel Circle" in *Season of Light*; and "At the Snakeskin Shoe
Outlet" in *Short Stuff*. A short version of "Christmas Sequins" is
forthcoming in *Adam's Media*. The author thanks the editors for
permission to reprint.

Cover art and design: Kristine Lowe-Martin

Jones, Judith Bader
Delta Pearls

ISBN: 0-9728708-2-2

Printed in the United States of America
First Edition

Sweetgum Press 713 Tyler Warrensburg, MO 64093

For Hildegarde and Dixie

CONTENTS

VENUS
1912
Kin Folk Ridge

Pain awakened Venus before the roosters called. The morning felt heavy with moisture from the river. Board-like she waited for the gripping pain to leave her stomach. She could bear it no longer when first light filtered through the filmy bedroom curtains. Venus gathered her gown around her, hunched forward, and padded to her parents' bedroom. Her hair hung to her waist in one soft braid. She knocked on their door.

"Papa, I'm sick. I hurt."

Joseph Christian opened the door, and in one swoop lifted his daughter and placed her across the foot of the bed. Venus pressed her hand over her stomach.

"Here, Papa. It hurts here."

"Lie still, let me see."

Joseph's dark hand pressed his daughter's pale stomach, here and there, examining this child as he had her brothers when they were ill. "I'll get you a cool cloth," he said, then spoke to her mother. "Her belly is a hard knot, Shay, and hot, too. Send to the Ridge for the doctor."

Venus crawled under the appliquéd quilt. The painful waves crested and fell. She watched her mother leave the room, silent as a white dove, her long gown sweeping the floor behind her.

It wasn't long before Doc Jeffers shuffled into the room.

1

Sometimes he came for the cows or the new babies, and sometimes he came for dinner. It was like that on a farm six miles from town.

"Let's have a look, girl. Hurts a lot?"

Venus opened her mouth to the wooden stick. The doctor looked and pressed and finally sat on the end of the bed. "Joseph, I think you might as well pack your bag. You can get her on the boat tonight. Take her on down to Memphis where she can get help. I swear it's her appendix."

"Does it have to come out?"

"Sooner, the better."

Shay Christian didn't look at her daughter. She straightened the pillows and bed covers. "Guess you'll take her, Joseph."

"Can she eat, Doc?" Joseph asked.

"Nothing much, water, tea or broth until they see her."

Venus sat up. The pain spread into her lower back. She searched her mother's face for a saving. Surely she wouldn't have to have an operation. That happened to old folks. The cows got operations when their legs caught in the fence and twisted. Their bones got pressed back into shape. She began to cry. Her mother's eyes never met hers.

The doctor left. Her mother packed. Her father barked, "Turn your head, girl. I have to dress."

Venus half closed her eyes. She couldn't help but see her father's backside in the light of early morning as he pulled on his trousers. "I'm scared," she said.

"Sure you are, but think on this. You're going to go all the way to Memphis, Tennessee, on one of the best night boats in the country—The Georgia. Did you know there'll be music and singing?"

Venus searched her father's face. His hazel eyes came alive when he talked about the boat. He pulled on his gray suit coat and slicked back his blond hair with rosewater. She liked the smell of him. His gold watch-chain glistened.

"Papa, it's still early. Doctor Jeffers said we'd go on the night boat."

"Eleven tonight we'll be at the landing. Right now, I'm going to town to borrow some money." He leaned down and kissed her cheek. Venus grabbed his arm and held on to her father for a moment before he pulled away.

She lay back on her parents' featherbed. Her mother returned with a basin of water. "Let's have a bit of a sponge off, Venus."

Venus reached for the rag in her mother's hand.

"You want me to help you, Venus, sick as you feel?"

"No. Thirteen-year-olds can wash. I'm not that sick. How long will I be there? Can't you take me to Memphis?"

Her mother was already at the door with her back turned. "Mercy me, no, your father is used to travel. Where I ever been? I need to stay home with your brothers."

The door closed before Venus could finish her sentence, "I'll be back in time to help you make the jelly."

The day heated up, but a breeze floated in from the orchard. A lost wasp darted from one corner of the room to the window. Venus watched him build his nest. His dizzy flight broke the monotonous spell of her wait. After her mother milked in the evening, she helped Venus dress in her best dark cotton. She re-braided Venus's fair hair and secured it with one of her own tortoise-shell combs.

Later that night, Venus's father carried her downstairs and put her on a cornhusk bed in the wagon. He gave her drops of bitters for the pain. Venus lay back in the wagon, looked up at the night. Stars outlined the heavenly skies. She knew her mother must have heard the wheels of the wagon creak as they turned onto the river-bottom road. Soft white roads, bleached in the moonlight, bore the wagon well, and the ride was smooth. Her father's man, Horizon, snapped leather straps across the buttocks of the four mules and spoke to them in a commanding but caring voice. Venus pulled her shawl up to her neck and whispered, "Lord, forgive me my sins and save me for I am not ready to die."

At the landing, they waited in darkness. Joseph and Horizon held up lanterns to signal the night boat. The waves of the murky Mississippi slapped the shoreline again and again, and somewhere a long way off they heard the deep-throated whistle of the approaching steamboat. The sound penetrated the woods of walnut trees and alarmed the wild dogs that raided the chicken coops of nearby farmers. An occasional blue heron dropped from the shoreline trees, flapped her wings, and fluttered high over the silky sandbar. The steamboat, glittering in gaslight, rounded the bend of one of the most crooked rivers in the world. The cast-iron bell rang to announce the boat's intent to stop. The pilot directed the vessel toward the bank and held it there with the engines running. A gangplank with cleats hinged to the bow of the boat lowered. A roustabout helped Horizon with their belongings and Joseph carried his daughter across the slippery, swaying plank and onto The Georgia. The clerk, a short man in dark colors and polished buttons, collected their four-dollar fare. The boat carried both cargo and passengers, and the captain directed them to their cabin on the second deck.

"Get settled in and come for a bit of supper—late fare, but plenty of beer, too."

"The girl is sick. Can she have some weak tea?"

The captain nodded as he left them in their cabin. Their berths were narrow shelves. Furnishings were sparse: a tin basin, pitcher, commode and kerosene lamp. A communal toothbrush hung chained to the wall.

"Do you feel like taking a bit of tea or broth?"

"My pain is all but gone. I think I would like sweet tea."

Joseph carried his daughter downstairs to the main saloon.

Venus

Venus was in a position to get a good view of everything. A grand mahogany staircase connected their deck with the dining area, which was itself in the saloon. Oval mirrors adorned the walls. A deep red-velvet carpet covered the floors. Venus was placed in a plush, gilded chair against the wall.

A huge table in the center of the room held a spread of foods: fish, roast beef, potatoes, rice, corn, fruit, nuts, puddings, and yellow cake. Her father brought her a steaming mug of tea and a bowl of chicken broth. His plate was laden with a variety of foods. He drank a hearty dark liquid that Venus thought must be whiskey or rum. His face flushed with the drink.

Venus leaned against the soft cushions in her chair. There were groups of men off to one side playing cards. Venus motioned for her father to come closer. She whispered, "Papa, see the men with the cards? They're sitting at tables that look like wooden coffins."

"They are coffins, but empty to be sure. They make dandy tables. I'm going to see if I can join one of those poker games." Joseph jingled the borrowed gold coins in his coat pocket and smiled at his daughter at the same time. "You can go to our cabin and rest."

"I don't want to rest. Can I sit here and watch you play?"

"Card games are no place for a young lady. Don't go telling your mother."

Venus nodded and crossed her heart with her left hand. Her father moved her to a chair closer to one of the groups.

"Room for one more?"

"Pull up a chair. We're playing three-card monte."

"I don't know how to play that one."

"No mind, mister. What's your name?"

"Christian, Joseph Christian."

The man with the black string tie and diamond ring nodded. "I'll call you Joe. I don't have much use for Christian. Puts me in mind of kneeling in church with my grandmother. My name is Devol."

Venus saw the cards. They didn't have numbers on them or kings or jacks. The pictures on these cards were of a man, a woman, or a baby.

Smoke circled the group. Devol said, "The idea of this game is I will shuffle the cards and lay them face down on the table. When it's your turn, you point to the card you think is the baby."

Devol's hands moved like those of a banker counting money. Venus watched as he did fancy shuffles. Each man set out gold or silver pieces on a bet that he could pick out the baby. Venus looked at her father. He ran his finger under his collar as the game proceeded. Some of the others lost their gold pieces, but her father continued to add to his tidy stack.

One of the men at the table let a card slip to his lap. The players didn't seem to notice. Then he covered the card with his hand and pitched it back onto the table. Her father noticed the card, too. He eyed that card as Devol placed it on the table alongside the others. Venus decided that one had to be a baby and that in some way the man had marked it and was a cheater.

"Your turn, Joe. Ante up."

"It's late. I'm laying all on this one."

Venus watched her father place his stacks of coins in the center of the table. He pointed to the card in the middle of the top line. The dealer paused, looked across the table at the man who had dropped a card in his lap, and turned the card over. It was no baby. The dealer swept all of the coins into his felt hat, and without so much as a word to the crimson-faced Joseph Christian, he and the others continued the game.

Venus smelled her father's rum-tainted breath when he picked her up to carry her to their cabin. She remained very still in his arms. This was a time to remain quiet, to wait like the quail by the river when they sense danger nearby. Her father didn't speak until he placed her in the narrow berth in the cabin.

"Get your rest. Do you need the pain drops?"

"No. It's a little ache now."

Venus lay back in her clothes with her shawl draped across her legs. She pretended to go to sleep, but all the while she watched her father as he removed his boots, set them outside the door, and shook the remaining coins from his leather pouch. Most of the money was gone, money to pay for her operation. He leaned forward with his hands to his face and swore to himself, "Damn bloody bastards."

Venus shut her eyes in fear, but felt the creaking comfort of her berth, a gentle rocking as the water lapped against weathered wood. She fell asleep with thoughts of her mother on their front porch at home, with the fireflies lighting the night. She heard her father toss and turn throughout the night until dawn crept in and the melodious whistles of The Georgia filled the foggy morning with a succession of notes. One long and two shorts announced the landing ahead, Memphis, Tennessee.

Venus waved good-bye to the boat's pilot seated in his glass-walled place, a sort of throne for the most prominent man on the boat. She wrinkled her nose at the stench of hot oil from the engine and mud from the streets at the landing. A roustabout handed her father their bag and found them a driver to take them to the hospital. Two horses drew their carriage, not a team of mules like on their farm.

"Settle in, miss. You might want this robe for cover. This fog chills a body's bones, even in summer."

Venus stared ahead to see morning coming down the road. Her father put his arm around her. She snuggled up against the rough fabric of his coat.

"What about the money, Papa? What will they say about that?"

Her father pulled her closer into his circle of warmth. "Don't fret. There will be a way."

Venus wondered if this was going to be another one of her secrets with her father. What a chore it was keeping quiet around so many things. But he was good, ever sweet, and the person she believed who loved her. He understood about her drawing, the pictures of her life. He seldom scolded when she shirked home duties to do her art-work. Not really work—art love. Her two brothers, Winfield and George B., didn't have it so good. He was sharp and tough with them. It was Mama she wished was closer, but Mama seemed to dart away, even in dreams.

The large brick hospital stood surrounded by cottonwoods and a clipped lawn. Stone lions guarded the entrance. Her father paid the driver and helped her out of the carriage. She walked a few steps before she doubled over with pain. She didn't argue when her father lifted and carried her to the door of the building. They used a brass knocker and waited until an old woman, wearing a starched, white apron, ushered them into a room with great reaching ceilings.

"What are you here for?" the woman asked.

Joseph drew in his breath, straightened his upper body and spoke in a booming voice. "Doc Jeffers from Kin Folk Ridge sent us. He says it's her appendix."

"Where's Kin Folk Ridge?"

Venus looked at the woman in surprise. Who didn't know where the Ridge was?

"It's about one hundred miles up the river in Missouri. We came on the boat."

Venus went with "white apron" and her father was left in the waiting room.

Once in the examining room, the nurse said, "Raise your arms." She helped Venus remove her dress and the petticoat with the frayed roses at the bottom. Venus crossed her arms to cover her beginning breasts. The woman loosened Venus's braid and brushed her hair with a few smooth strokes. She slipped a cotton gown over Venus's head and helped her onto a high table.

Dr. Brooks, a short man in his middle years, entered the room. He washed his hands in a stark basin. "What have we here, a midget? Ah, no, a wee lass. What's wrong with you?"

"I have stomach pains."

The doctor pressed on Venus's stomach and when he removed his hands, she felt a jolt of pain. She cried out.

"There now, I think you need my help. Nurse, find her parents so I can speak to them."

"My father is here."

Joseph pushed open the door without being summoned. "I have no money to pay. I'll get it later, pay you on time."

Dr. Brooks looked at Venus's father. "Mr. Christian, it's our policy to collect payment for our services. This isn't a charity place. Your daughter needs an operation to remove her appendix. You look honest enough. I can consider taking her as a research patient. There's no charge to research patients. They receive surgery from our staff in training, under my watchful eye. When you're financially able, perhaps you can make a contribution to our medical school or to the Children's Service."

Joseph's face relaxed. He appeared younger. He smiled, swallowed, and shook his head in agreement. "You won't be sorry, Dr. Brooks. I'll make it good when the crop is in. Cotton looks good, beans too."

"We'll operate in the morning, soon as the tests are done and the students see her. There's a boarding house down the street where you can get some rest and get chicken and dumplings, too. Venus, you go with Nurse Gayle to our Children's Service."

"Don't go, Papa. I'm scared."

"I'll be back this evening and for your operation in the morning." With these words, her father hesitated, and then reached into his pocket. He pressed something smooth into Venus's hand.

Venus looked down to see her father's pocket watch. She opened the cover. The face was white porcelain with Roman numeral hands. A miniature portrait on the opposite side was of a young woman wearing a cameo. Venus recognized the face of her mother. She clutched the watch. She held something of her father and also her mother who seemed so far away, so grown up and beautiful, and as now, so out of reach when Venus needed her.

The Children's Service was a huge room filled with narrow beds. Starched curtains hung suspended from the ceiling to be drawn around individual beds. Venus was assigned to a bed next to a girl who immediately said, "You'll hate it here. Lamps out at eight. Can't do anything but rest. Why are you here?"

"Appendicitis—an operation."

"Oh, I had that a couple of weeks ago. I'm going home soon. I don't have family—I mean, a mother or a father."

Venus looked at the girl. "Are you all alone?"

"No, I live in the Children's Home over on Elm."

"What's that?"

"A place for kids like me that weren't wanted by their mothers."

Venus felt a sense of shock and scare. "I never heard of a mother who didn't want her child."

"What kind of mother you got?"

Venus was quiet for a moment. She thought about her mother with her tight black braids pinned up close to her head. "My mother is a proper woman with a lot of chores and two boys aside of me to look out for." A deep sadness gripped Venus when she finished speaking. It was as though her voice went out of her all at once. She straightened her bed covers and adjusted the sleeves of her gown.

"Where is your proper mother?" the girl asked. "You're here at death's door. Where is she?"

"She's at home. My father is here, down the way at a boarding house." The words, *proper mother . . . proper mother,* reeled in her mind.

The skinny red-headed girl laughed as she held her hand over her stomach. "Maybe he's out for some rum. That's the likes of most men."

"What would you know about my father? He's a dear man, and for your information he never takes rum." Venus shocked herself with the ease of her lie. Hadn't her own father drunk rum and gambled their funds away on the boat? Venus couldn't help herself. She said, "I'm sorry you don't have a mother or a father to love you. That must be very painful inside your heart, but that doesn't allow you to throw sticks at my folks. Wait until you meet my father before you decide anything. I'm tired. I hurt. I'm going to go to sleep."

Venus closed her eyes, but she heard the girl next to her get out of bed and come closer. The girl pulled the cover over Venus's shoulders and said in a small voice, "I'm Rose, Rose McKinney, Irish and proud."

Venus remembered her father telling her that some of the roustabouts on the boat were Irish, but not treated as well as the colored men who usually held that post. She sank into a light sleep with the image of the girl with red curls and green eyes standing guard by her bedside.

Later in the day, Dr. Brooks awakened Venus. "These are my students," he said, "doctors studying to learn anatomy and conditions. Tomorrow they'll be in the round to remove your appendix. One of these scholars will assist me."

Venus looked at the sea of faces around her. "Papa says I'll be asleep and I won't feel anything."

Rose McKinney laughed and stuck her head around the drawn curtain and groaned.

"Stop it, Rose," the doctor said, "don't scare this girl."

Venus introduced Rose to her father when he came after

supper. Rose was quiet, but she listened to every word they spoke. When the nurse came into the room, Rose became quarrelsome. "No, I won't straighten my things. I won't walk to the day room. Leave me alone, you old biddy."

"I know what you're about, Rose McKinney," the nurse said, not too harshly at all. "You don't want to leave us. That's it, isn't it?"

Rose looked at Nurse Gayle and then she screamed and swore until Dr. Brook's assistant came and gave her stomach bitters to quiet her.

Venus's father went to the side of the girl's bed and straightened her pillows. "What words from a young girl! If you were my daughter you would curtail that talk. You need someone to teach you the ways of becoming a lady."

Venus watched her father tend the girl. His eyes changed colors from green to gray, and his words spilled out like from an old clucking hen.

The next morning, they rolled Venus into a cold room with bright gaslights. She heard voices in the background, voices that must be floating in the back pasture. "Over here, pet. That's a girl. Take a deep breath." And that was all, until she woke up to the strangest wretched smell. Nurse Gayle helped her rid her stomach of meager contents. The June day collected in the window with prisms of sunshine, but Venus shivered cool and damp. In the evening, she at last realized where she was. Her father was by the bed, stiff and wax-like.

The doctors came to her bedside, a fortress in white. Dr. Brooks talked for all of them.

"It was a foul appendix. Lucky for her, it's gone. Unfortunately, there's more. The uterus was taken, too."

"Her womb? Whatever for?"

Dr. Brooks looked down. He leaned closer to her father. "It was a terrible mistake. The assistant didn't know. He thought things were different in there. He sliced it in error. He couldn't stop the bleeding. He took it."

"Why didn't you stop him? How can this be?"

"I was called to help another, a fellow burnt badly in a barn fire."

"I ought to by well beat you to a pulp. You've sucked her womanhood from her. My grace, my child . . ."

Her father's face grew red, turned bright the way it did in planting time when he stayed in the sun too long. His rage came on quickly and left quickly. His sobs filled the room. Venus shut her eyes. She had never seen her father cry. It frightened her. Her womb . . . was he crying for her womb? The pain in her body rose above the thinking part of her. "I hurt."

Venus faded in and out of sleep for the next few days. She vaguely saw the doctors come and go; their hands gouged and pressed her until she awakened herself with a single scream that fragmented her thoughts. She returned to reality to see her father by her bed in wrinkled clothes. He smelled of sweat.

"Venus, I'm going back to the farm, but will be back to get you in a couple of weeks when you're strong enough to come home."

Before he could say more, Rose, in the next bed, interrupted him. "Give her the box, the present. Venus, I thought you'd never get waked enough to open this up." She slipped to the floor, hefted the box, and pushed it toward Venus.

Venus's father took the box with trembling hands. "I'll open it for you."

"Who's it from?"

"Nurse Gayle brought it yesterday. Said it was from one of the young doctors."

Rose stood by the bed. "Well, Venus, look at this. It looks like a real live baby."

Venus tried to see inside the box. Her father lifted the baby doll. He smoothed its long dress and handed it to his daughter.

"Oh, Papa, she's the most beautiful doll I've ever seen. She does look exactly like a newborn baby."

Rose was quiet at first. "Yes, exactly like a real live baby. And then she looked at Venus's father and said, "Aren't you going to tell her?"

"Tell me what, Papa?"

"There's something we need to talk about. They made a mistake. When they took the appendix, they also took out your womb."

"Oh. I remember hearing that."

Her father wiped his face. The lines in his forehead stayed.

"You won't be having any babies of your own, Venus, not ever. I mean, when you are grown and married there won't be any womb inside to carry babies to birth." Her father's voice was a high pitch. "Do you understand me? Your mother should be here to explain these matters."

"Did Dr. Brooks do it?"

"No. One of the students learning the trade made a mistake."

Her father left later that day to go home to work in the hay. Venus looked at the doll beside her and remembered where she had seen one like it. Ward's catalogue, the wish book at home by the sideboard. It was a Sweet Dreams baby. Way too costly for Santa Claus to bring for Christmas. She patted the doll and fell asleep.

Two weeks passed. Venus worried about her father coming to get her, traveling on the boat. Rose and she dressed and waited together. Venus heard the sound of tapping coming down the hall, the kind of sound her mother's boots made, small clicking steps. When Venus looked up, her mother was at the door. She stood in hesitation.

"Mama," Venus cried out, "you've come for me? You traveled

all the way up the river on the boat?"

Venus's mother held out her arms and then in quick steps she took Venus in her arms and held her in a rocking motion. "I am so grateful to see you. You look well and strong. I missed you at the house."

"Is it time to put up the peaches?"

"And who have we here? Is this your new friend, Rose?"

For the first time, Venus saw her friend with deep flushed cheeks, crying soundlessly. Venus said, "Oh, Mama, Rose wants to come home with us . . . for a visit."

"Is that so, Rose?"

Rose nodded.

"Venus's father has already arranged such a visit, and I hope you will decide to stay past this summer. Much longer."

They were ready to leave. Venus picked up the Sweet Dreams baby doll and put her in the chair by the bed, but that didn't seem right. She moved the doll and placed her on top of the bedside table, but still the doll didn't sit right. At last, she placed her on the bed with her head on the pillow. She put her shawl over the doll, patted her, turned and left the room.

Missouri Bootheel Cold

Zero arrived.
Farms froze
like barb wire.
Windows rattled
and straddled
howling wind.
Iron bedsteads
chilled time.
Clocks stopped.
Everyone slept
with someone
to steal body heat
at the dark end
of winter on
Missouri farms.

MORNINGS AND MAMA

I heard country music in the mornings, moaning love songs
from the likes of Eddie Arnold and Roy Acuff. I cuddled in bed
under a grandma quilt with the cat at my feet. My iron bedstead
was cool to touch, but ugly in the eyes of someone young like
me.

The country singers dipped in and out of love with
monotonous lyrics, but the swaying guitar sounds were as
comforting as Mama herself.

Mama came to Missouri a new sixteen, a bride, and a stranger
to mosquitoes and hillbilly music. She was unaccustomed to
outdoor toilets and temperamental sows. It was her habit in the
morning to sit at the chrome kitchen table, sipping coffee colored
with cream. I saw her there morning after morning and heard
the sounds of Eddie Arnold. Mama listened and Eddie sang his
heart out for his radio audience. I thought she seemed dreamy
like staring off across the room. What was she seeing, I wondered.
She was religious-looking, like a choir person at our Methodist
church on Sunday, mouth moist and eyes steamed up and wide
open. Her hair resembled tassels of field corn. Her eyes were
blue or green or gray depending on how much light they found.
Her skin was olive-colored and soft from Pond's cream.

One morning, Mama was dancing in the kitchen. She didn't

see me standing in the doorway. She held out her arms to a partner who wasn't there. She turned around, moving two steps at a time, back and forth over linoleum flowers. Her chin tilted high, eyes closed, and her lips moved to mouth the words in a song. I cleared my throat and entered the room. The dreamy look faded, but she smiled and opened her arms to me. We danced. Mama hummed, low like, and my feet hurried to follow her lead.

The dancing Mama I loved stopped abruptly. She was looking out of the window. I turned to see my father coming across the broom-swept yard. I heard his step on the porch and the banging of our screen door. He came in wearing boots heavy with Mississippi River mud.

"Pour me a cup of coffee and turn that blasted racket off!"

Mama flicked the radio knob with her left hand and reached for a coffee cup with the right. She stood tall, but worked quickly.

My father slapped the table. "How about a biscuit?"

Mama smoothed her apron and quietly folded her arms across her bosom.

"With a little sorghum. That would be ever so sweet."

My mother smiled and said, "That's more like it."

She served my father pale biscuits and we watched him lower his head to meet his fork. Mama ate in a different manner, with backbone straight and a cloth napkin on her lap. She took tiny bites and no one could even hear her crunch celery.

My father tilted back in his chair and its legs left digging rings on the floor covering. Thirty-nine rings clustered around his chair. Mama called them worry rings.

"Beans look fine, real good stand, not a weed in them!"

My mother's face became an ornament in a plain kitchen. She wore her something-good-is-going-to-happen face.

"The bean-crop money will just barely cover our debts, so don't get fancy ideas."

Mama nodded. Silence hung around.

"Oh, sugar," he said, "there will be enough for you a dress, some shoes, and a trip to Memphis." He turned to me. "And you . . . You're going to get a red bike."

I smiled. I wanted to say words, lots of words to show him my happy insides, but he was already on his way out the door.

Mama and I cleaned up the kitchen while Eddie Arnold sang us another song. We didn't talk, didn't have to. We were weaving in and out of the music in a new dress, riding a red bike all the way to Memphis, Tennessee, living dreams that could open and spill all over our life in the Missouri Bayou.

The Petrified Man and My New York Grandmother

Every single time my New York grandmother came to visit us in Missouri, trouble followed. She'd unpack her better dresses and hang them on my sister's side of the closet and slip into her no-nonsense black pumps and starched housedresses just in time to start dinner. She always let our Letha go home early so she could have the whole kitchen to herself. Letha never minded. She'd been cooking for us all our days, and I guess she liked a kitchen rest. I loved my grandmother's northern cooking. I knew for six weeks I would be spared the agony of grits and mustard greens. I looked forward to gingerbread and molasses cookies, lemon meringue pie, and angel food cake with confectionary sugar icing. I missed Letha's fried chicken and soft biscuits and sorghum, but the change was interesting. The food wasn't at all the misery.

My grandmother had one issue she loved to hammer my father with. It was about the petrified man in the back of the Morley funeral home. He was in this wood-box affair that stood up on one end. He had been standing there all of my life, and my father said he had been there for as long as he could remember. The whole world knew about him. All the school kids slipped in the back screen door to look him over ever so often, especially about the beginning of school when the little kids first started walking home. They would file in and stand huddled together in that shadowy half-light. The petrified man wore a towel draped around his middle, and the real ornery kids would lift the towel so that everyone could see a naked petrified man!

This particular Sunday, my grandmother waited until my father had his mouth half-full of one of her special dishes before she started in about the likes of our town and our people. "George B., I can't understand a man of your background and education staying here and exposing your wife and lovely daughters to this culture."

"Grandma," I said, "what background are you talking about? Daddy always said he was a poor country boy raised up in a dog-trot house." I loved to get my grandmother's goat about my dad's background. She was from some aristocrats in New York, blue bloods, she said. I'm not sure about that part. I bet her blood was as red as my dad's. "Daddy, didn't you go to an agricultural school in Marble Hill when you were young?"

"Sure did, but you know, I got so homesick that after the first month I came back home to the farm. The next time I went to college, it was Arkansas. I took a cow with me to be sure I had fresh milk, but I never stayed there for too long either."

"Was that your education?"

"Formally, yes, but my real education came from reading and studying on my own."

"You mean like *The Democrat Argus* and *The Memphis Commercial Appeal*?"

By the time my father finished talking about his education, my grandmother was coloring up from pressing her lips together so tightly. But that didn't last long at all. She gave me one of her stern looks, and with one swift movement, she cleared away the last piece of pie on the table, the piece I hoped would be mine before bedtime. Meanwhile, my sister Dixie Lou, who was two years older than me, was kicking blue blotches on my legs. That was her signal for me to shut up.

21

After the grown-ups drank their coffee, my grandmother took a soul-searching breath and began again in a very sweet voice that promised to rise up sharply in a funnel cloud. "George, can't you go to the mayor and get him to remove that man from the funeral home? He would listen to you. I know he would. After all, this is 1943, and things have changed."

"Mother Taylor," my father said, "and just what do you want me to suggest they do with him?"

"Why bury him, of course."

"You want me to tell the mayor he ought to bury the petrified man, because my mother-in-law finds it offensive we keep him on display?"

"Bury him in the Methodist cemetery."

"You want him buried with the city founders? The Methodist cemetery? Good grief!" he bellowed. "Woman, do you know that even I won't be allowed in there?"

I interrupted. "Daddy, what makes him so stiff?"

"You see, George, your own daughter doesn't know the moral horror of this situation. Why don't you tell her something about the ethical and moral crime committed against this poor soul, this petrified man." She turned to me. "No, my dear child, he was not born petrified."

My father ran his hand across his balding head and cleared his throat. "A long time ago," he said, "This man was probably a vagrant in our town and died on the bottle. No one knew him, and no one wanted to pay for his funeral, so the funeral home took him in, so to speak, and petrified him with some special fluids. They stood him up in the back room."

My grandmother smoothed the cotton folds in her apron, leaned forward and said, "You see, girls, he was a conversation piece, an oddity for people to gawk at. George B., I want you to tell them the other story."

My father's face paled and his mouth drooped at the corners.

He fussed with his gold wedding band and tipped back in his chair, studying the air in front of him. "Some say he was hanged, lynched, and left on the road for the buzzards. Some farmer probably took him to the undertaker for want of a better way."

My father left the table without finishing his lemon pie. I skipped after him, and slipped under his arm and matched my walk to his. The sadness sank so low on my father that even his work pants seemed to sag. For the first time, I understood what my grandmother meant about our town and our people. I ran ahead of my sorrowful father and into the beginning of night. The mosquitoes came with us.

The moon rose round and precious, and the shadows of the twilight chased the last saved fragment of day. I slipped into my tire swing that hung from the largest cottonwood tree in our yard and pushed my knees and extended my legs as I soared. Gliding so high, I saw the Mississippi River mounding the bend to roll by our town that hid in the fold of night. And then I cried.

Soon after that night, the petrified man disappeared from the back of the funeral home. No one knows what happened to him for sure. A small sign appeared in the funeral home window. It stood propped against the rose-colored drapes that covered the tall windows:

$50 REWARD for information leading
to the return of the petrified man,
property of Morley Funeral Home.
Call 836 W during working hours.

During the same week, on a Sunday, a large mound appeared on the back of our east-forty. The dirt, dark river-bottom loam, was newly turned, but it wasn't planting time.

My grandmother never mentioned the petrified man again. She never had to. I remembered him. He wasn't a tall man. He was a small-boned man with a white towel draped around his middle. That towel reflected all of the light in the dusty back room of the funeral home and somehow became iridescent against his black skin.

DECEMBER ROSES
1937

"Roses say I love you." I know that must be right because I heard it on the *Guiding Light* radio show. Where could I find roses blooming in winter? No blossoms in anyone's garden. Rose bushes living in December were naked, thorny sticks.

I heard Mama playing the radio, some New Orleans station with nothing but Bourbon Street Blues. I wondered why we didn't have much Christmas music at our house. Mama didn't seem to get into Christmas until the first week in December when she started making her Million Dollar Fudge. She'd wrap the candy in butcher's paper and Sammy Joe and I would stand down there on Water Street outside the Honey Dripper Bar and sell it to Christmas shoppers or workers getting off riverboats.

I wondered if shoppers might know where I could find roses. It was beginning to snow, dainty flakes at first, but before long the whole waterfront turned holy white with snow and silence interrupted only by barge foghorns,

"Roses, do you know who might have any this time of year?" I asked each person who stopped to buy fudge. Some folks didn't answer, but one of the men who got off the boat seemed to have time to talk.

"Kid, why are you looking for roses?"

"Roses say I love you."

"Aren't you kind of young to be saying 'I love you' with flowers? Your fudge is very good. Who made it?"

"My mom. It's her Million Dollar Fudge recipe."

"I could sell a whole lot of this candy on the boat, and in places where we dock, all the way to New Orleans. Your mama make much of this?"

"Yes, sir. Is it warm down in New Or-leans?"

"Lot warmer than this far north."

"You got flowers blooming down there?"

"We got anything anybody can dream of in New Orleans. I tell you what, you get your mama to make me about one-hundred pounds of fudge and I will see that you get some flowers."

Mama made the fudge after she borrowed money from our neighbor to buy the ingredients. "Milk and butter is costly enough," she said, "but sugar, well, that's way high and scarce as bananas."

Sammy Joe and I hauled the fudge down to the waterfront the next Saturday in his red wagon and waited for the boat, but it didn't come that day at all. On Sunday, after church, we went right back down there. The fudge froze even though we covered it with feed sacks.

After school on Monday, we again went to the dock. Miss Hagedorn, an old maid who owned River Cafe, came by and said, "Boats can't pass through the river ice up north in St. Louis. Won't get here till it thaws. What you boys got in your wagon under all that sacking?"

"Fudge. Mama made a lot of it for this man who works on the boat."

I couldn't look at her, because I knew my disappointed tears were coming.

"Well, why don't you sell your fudge in my cafe?"

"No, we can't. The man promised me flowers, roses from New Orleans, if we could bring the fudge."

"Roses, landsakes. The only kind of roses anyone will find this time of year are dried and pressed in some old love letters. You might as well get some money for the candy, after all your mother's work."

Folks at the cafe bought our fudge and asked for more. When we got home, our Mama's eyes lit up like Christmas candles at the coins we stacked up on the kitchen table. Before we put away the wagon, I found a small paper bag from the River Cafe under the feed sacks. Inside was one pale, dried rosebud pressed in a faded card that said "I love you" written in perfect cursive letters.

I propped the rose up on the kitchen table, right next to Mama's coffee cup, where she would find it first off on Christmas morning. I kept the card in my desk drawer, underneath my tablet, and wondered who had ever loved old Miss Hagedorn. Maybe he was a riverboat captain who chose to go on down to New Orleans for good. That Christmas, Sammy Joe and I found our stockings half-full of shiny coins, the kind that Santa Claus must keep on hand for kids like us who know the meaning of a dime and understand the language of roses.

Peace be in Your Heart

"Now Em, don't go bothering your father none."

Em left her mother in the kitchen and swept up the stairs with the ease of a cat. In her arms she carried two magic-skin dolls, her babies. She avoided the groaning steps, moved from one side of the stairwell to the other until she reached the upper hallway. Her parents' bedroom door was closed. The doorknob felt black and smooth. She turned it ever so carefully, opened the door and slipped in. A lamp in the corner made a little light. The moon looking in the window lit the remaining dark corners in the room.

Em sat in her mother's stuffed chair by the window. She hugged her dolls, one under each arm.

"Daddy, do you see these babies? I am going to put them to bed. They are so tired." Em laid her dolls on the bed. She whispered, "Hush, babies, I will make you a story. Once upon a time, a mom and dad got married. They lived in a gingerbread house with a shaggy cat and many babies. They had happy love. There, there . . . that is enough stories. Good-night sweet babies. Sleep well and peace be in your hearts."

Em kissed her dolls with wet lips drawn up like a drawstring purse. She frowned. "Daddy, what does 'peace be in your heart' mean?" Em rested her hand over her heart and walked closer to the window. She waved at the moon and clasped her hands.

"Oh, it's snowing. Oh, come and see. The barn is turning white. The mare is wearing a frosty tail. Tomorrow, will you make me a snowman and pull me in my sled that Grandpa made? Remember last year the snow rested here for a long time, and Mama said our wood was counting few? I think there's a lot of wood now with the maple tree that gave out and died. Tomorrow I can do snow angels out back. Why do they call them snow angels? Is that what angels are really like, with wings?"

Em flapped her arms in the thin air of the winter evening. Her breath misted the window and drew a curtain on the snow scene below. She sat in her mother's stuffed chair again, and this time she clutched her knees under her chin. Her eyes opened full circle and she smiled.

"You know, Mrs. Fischer, my teacher, says I'll learn to read when I'm ready. Sometimes the letters fade into each other. They give me a sweat sorting them out. Mrs. Fischer says I'm quick and reading will come. I know all of the pictures in the book. I want to show you the one with the sailing ship. Can you ride the water like that in your old fishing boat?

"Daddy, darling, the singing's on the radio now. I'll turn it on low like. How's that? And by the way, when you wake up, there are some things I've been meaning to ask you. I hope I didn't disturb your sleep. Mama says you are sleeping and I am not supposed to bother you. I see you are sleeping good. No, no, don't bother to wake up to kiss me good-night. I've got a whole mess of kisses right here in my pocket. Good-night, Daddy. I hope it snows all night."

Em left her father and stood in the upstairs hallway. She heard her mother in the kitchen downstairs. The back door slammed. She felt the chill of winter rush up the stairwell. She heard a man's voice and her mother's laughter. Em ran down the stairs so fast that she forgot to watch for groaning steps.

"Uncle Mikel! Uncle Mikel! Oh, Uncle Mikel!"

She streaked across the linoleum flowers on the kitchen floor and stretched out her arms to surround his middle. She tilted her head back to look up at her favorite uncle's bearded face.

"You are really cold and wet. You're wearing snow in your hair."

The smiling man squatted to meet his niece face to face. He stroked her tawny hair with one hand and puckered his lips for kisses. Em put her arms around his neck and laid her head against his plaid jacket. The cold of him brought shivers to her body. The beating of his heart matched her own.

"I am going to stay all night, and in the morning we will build the king of snowmen. Your old Uncle Mikel knows how to make a super snowman. I will show you how to do it."

Tears rolled down Em's cheeks. Her uncle wiped her tears with his hand and carried her to a rocker by the cook stove. He held her in his arms until her eyelids lowered and she smiled in sleep.

"Peace be in your heart," he said. "I love you."

LETHA'S CAGED MONKEYS

Letha twisted Dixie Lou's long curls around her finger with a hairbrush until they hung down her back in perfect harmony. Ruth Ann was ready and waiting for the old woman to finish her sister's hair. Letha always liked to stand back, "my-oh-meeing," after she added the rose-colored bow to the back of Dixie Lou's hair. Ruth Ann wore a Dutch-bob which required just a quick once-over. Letha oohed and aahed just as much when she brushed the straight bobbed hair as when she attended to Dixie's curls. She added a little spittle from her generous mouth to the bangs to make them lie flat.

The girls wore their Sunday patent-leather shoes which Dixie Lou loved to pretend were for tap dancing on the polished kitchen linoleum. Letha hung her apron behind the kerosene stove and stationed her large black purse over a well-padded arm.

"Guess we're ready, girls."

Letha led the way. The girls walked behind her until they came to Water Street. Then they walked side by side. The street was layered with fine pale dirt and gravel.

"Oh, Letha, my shoes don't glow anymore," Dixie complained.

"No matter. When we get there I'll dust them off with my kerchief."

Dixie Lou smiled at Letha. "I'm gonna get you some special shoes for Christmas so you'll be able to walk faster like me and

Ruth Ann."

"Pshaw, child! I don't need no special shoes to make me move faster. What I need is a car to ride me around, but never mind cars and shoes. I'm taking you to see something you've never seen in all of your ten years. Monkeys! Just you wait . . . cages and cages of monkeys who can move like the spirit of the Lord."

"Letha, where'd this bar place get monkeys in cages?"

"Don't say 'bar place' lest your daddy think I lost all of my senses taking an eight and ten year old to a drinking house. Right name of this place is Edward's Paradise, and we're only going into the back room to see the monkeys. Lord only knows where they come from. See, like in the encyclopedia under M, big doe eyes on them so full of velvet makes you want to weep and touch their softness. They have long tails for swinging and sliding."

"Are they like cats, Letha?"

"Oh, no! They're wise little fellows with honest-to-goodness hands which reach out the bars at you for something. But then, they're so scared they run back before you can touch them."

Letha turned off Water Street and onto an alley leading to the back entrance of Edward's Paradise.

"Edward's Paradise!" Dixie Lou placed her hands on her hips as she stopped in front of a screen door, more door than screen. "I'm not going into a place looks like a rat hole."

Ruth Ann grabbed the faint cloth of Letha's dress and followed her into the dark musty place which her sister labeled a rat hole. Dixie Lou glanced to the left and to the right and hurried after her sister. The trio stood in the darkness of a room which held numerous crates and one naked light bulb on a long cord. Letha grasped the chain and turned on the light.

"Monkeys? Where are they, Letha?"

Letha scanned the tarred and papered walls, yellowed with age. There were no monkeys. Music from the front of Edward's Paradise Club drifted into the empty back room that turned black again, became a hollow darkness when Letha jerked the light cord. Letha rushed out into the sun of summer with the spit-and-polished girls on her heels.

"Sun sure is heating up. Makes my eyes smart," Letha said, as she removed her kerchief and wiped her eyes clean.

Dixie Lou looked at Ruth Ann, shrugged her shoulders and put her index finger to her lips. Ruth knew about that. Meant don't say a word.

Two days later, Letha headed toward Water Street again.

"You think she's going to see about those monkeys?"

"Yeah, Ruth, but she'll come get us when she finds them."

When Letha returned, she sat in the kitchen and rocked with her hands folded in her lap. She wore a long face that belonged to someone else. She held her kerchief knotted in her hand and dabbed her eyes and nose. No, Letha didn't see the monkeys that day, the girls decided.

It wasn't long after that Letha took sick and stayed in her bed in the room behind the kitchen. "Get Brother Samuel," she said over and over until the girl's father drove across town to find Letha's minister. He came to the house every few days to visit with Letha. Ruth Ann sat in the kitchen and rocked back and forth while Brother Samuel read from his book. Letha gave out with a lot of "Amens" when the preacher paused in his reading.

On Friday, Dixie Lou said, "Ruth, you and I have to go see Letha's caged monkeys."

"But, Dixie, they aren't there!"

"Never mind, Ruth. You get your patents on and we're going."

The girls walked in solemn silence to Water Street. They ran all of the way down the rusty tin-can graveyard of an alley that led to Edward's Paradise. Hand in hand, they entered the back room. They were too short to reach the chain on the light, so they stood in the murky room until their eyes adjusted to the darkness.

"There they are!"

Ruth held onto her sister and peered around.

"Look at that lively little fellow swinging on a bar. And over there, I see one holding out his hand. There's one dancing to Paradise music."

Ruth stared into the darkness. She didn't see any monkeys because there were none. She could feel Dixie's heartbeat pounding in her hand. Their sweat glued them together. Ruth knew at that moment they were sisters, molded into one secret, one flesh, one heart, and one sacred lie.

Dixie Lou led the way out and chattered all the way down Water Street. "Was something better to see than the movies in Memphis, don't you think, Ruth? I mean just about the best thing I ever saw. Those monkeys are wise and can even dance."

Ruth nodded her head in total agreement.

Dixie ran ahead into their house to find Letha. "Letha, we saw them," she yelled. "We saw your monkeys in the cages. They were getting ready to ride the ferry down to Tennessee. They were b-e-a-u-t-i-f-u-l."

Letha raised her head from her bed. Her feet were wrapped in kerosene-dipped muslin to ease the aching. The room smelled strong. "You saw the monkeys?"

"Yes, we saw them. Their little hands reached out, and some did tricks. Those monkeys are moving to a circus where they will live in a big open tent." Dixie's eyes grew large with the telling.

Letha's mouth opened wide as her head fell back and she laughed a low, rolling, musical sound. Wrinkle lines lifted as she smiled and laughed and cried clear, silent tears. Ruth Ann put her arms around Letha to gather as much of the softness as she could hold. Dixie tapped across the kitchen floor.

Letha said, "See, children, I told you I had something to show you like you never saw before. Old Letha knows a thing or two in this world. You aren't ever going to forget Letha's caged monkeys."

Dixie Lou looked at Ruth Ann and said, "No, we aren't ever going to forget."

Ruth looked at the old woman and smiled. She buried her head into the warm softness of the woman's neck, and felt Letha's fingers smooth her hair one strand at a time, adding a little spit to make the hair stay down smooth and flat.

After that, Letha took to getting well. The next time Brother Samuel came around, Ruth followed him to the front door.

"Brother Samuel, she said, addressing him as she had heard Letha do. "Do you know Edward's Paradise Club?"

He nodded, yes.

"Did you ever see monkeys in cages in the back room? Letha cares a lot about monkeys and my sister knows them real good. I think my sister loves them."

The preacher stood in silence.

"Brother Samuel, what happened to those caged monkeys?"

"Why, they died . . . a long time ago."

"Why?"

"Don't you know you can't cage a living thing?"

"Oh . . ."

"By the way, your Letha is getting better. She's not going to die for a long spell. She told me today she felt good enough to tap dance in the kitchen in a pair of patent-leather pumps."

Ruth Ann smiled. "You know my sister knows how to tap dance real good. I'm going to learn to do that right after I look in the encyclopedia under M. Don't you think monkeys are beautiful?"

"Sure they are. Living creatures are like that."

SHADY

Shady was like that. He had big ideas. Dreams and designs twirled around his head like a tilt-a-whirl under all that wooly hair. It must have been the terrible heat that fueled his last project. Ruth and I were melting in the front yard. Not one breath of air was up, but you could smell the dust from the road. No rain for weeks.

"What do you think Shady is up to?" I asked.

"Probably just none of our business," my sister Ruth snapped back.

"I think he's doing something secret. Remember when he made that little riverboat in the barn? How about the time he painted all those eggs with yellow paint? We thought for sure we had a golden goose. Let's follow him this afternoon when he takes off. He always heads out toward the old barn near the Trotter shack when his chores are finished."

"Now, Dee Dee, you know Shady don't want no kids spying on his doings. He'll get Papa to swat us good for being busybodies."

"Maybe he's building a castle this time with a real drawbridge and a moat. Last week he hauled all those bags of cement and some fine pine sticks and boards, and Lord only knows what else of Papa's he carted off."

"Shady would never steal from Papa. He only borrows from

time to time when Papa's not looking. Papa really sees everything out of the back of his head, everything we all do. Probably he even watches God at work."

"Sssh, Ruth. Papa hears all, too."

Ruth looked to the left and to the right across the empty wheat field. We both giggled until we saw Shady hop on the wagon with the two mules hitched up. He stood with the reins in his hand and brought a smart slap to the rumps of the mules with one end of the shiny leather in his hand. We heard his "gat-up" as he passed us on his way toward the river. His bare back shone in the sun, sweat rolled from his black body. We just sat there under the tree and tried to fan the heat with big cottonwood leaves.

Finally I said, "Come on, Ruth, let's follow him."

We walked down the road in a trail cut by Shady's wagon, a road that changed with each surge of the river's breeze. The fields caked in the drought, but the road sifted sand upon itself and lay in mounds. That road had been known to give up lost horseshoes, dried flowers, and smooth pebbles as round as the moon. Snakes slept in the road until roused by wagons or wild dogs that cruised by in the night looking to steal our chickens.

Ruth and I crept around behind the old barn. The mules stood tied, and Shady, for heaven's sake, was lying in a pool of water.

"Well, look at that. It's a concrete hole, like a real bathtub. He's run water from that pipe, hooked up to a pump. That pool must be two feet deep and Shady's lying there like in a bathtub in the ground. All that cement was to make himself a bathtub in the yard. Ruth, Shady doesn't have a stitch of clothes on."

"Of course not. Nobody takes a bath with clothes on."

"Someday, Mama says, we're going to have a house with a real bathtub."

"Yeah, I know, but Mama also thinks we'll get to shop in

Memphis. Papa says that isn't so and that Mama is lucky to ride over to Portageville to sell eggs or down to Blytheville for her doctor visits."

"Look, he's using Mama's soap to wash his back."

Shady rubbed his arms and legs with the soap and lay back in the water with his wet head resting on a ridge of the new tub. His muscles swelled as the water floated over his body. He closed his eyes and floated from side to side.

I looked at Ruth and we both turned to stare at Shady. "Do you think all men look like Shady?"

Ruth was silent for a moment and then she said, "Men are men and women are women. Shady is a fine specimen. That's what his woman Cora says. Guess we're looking at a fine specimen. Cross my heart and hope to die, I'll never tell. Cross your heart, too. Never tell about Shady. It's not nice for us to be looking."

I said, "Well, I'm going to look real good so I know about fine specimens."

Ruth took one final look and said, "Let's go home."

But by the new tub something dark moved. The thing twirled close to the ground and slithered closer to the tub, toward the rippling water. My heart thumped hollow thumps, even in my ears. Ruth's eyes were big. Her mouth opened.

"Shady . . . Watch out for the snake!"

I covered my eyes at first, but then I watched Shady turn to his side. He looked hollow-eyed. Then he was up and out of that tub. The snake crawled in and he crawled out. Shady grabbed his pants with one hand and a board with the other. He raised the board and beat at the snake, and then we heard him say, "Oh shoot."

From the depths of nowhere, Papa appeared. He looked at us. Then he turned to Shady who had one leg in his pants. He looked next at the oval pool with rounded corners and smooth sides.

Shady gathered his wits and his composure and said, "I made it for you, Boss. For these hot days. I just tested it out to make sure it didn't leak."

Papa said, "I'll water the cows here."

Now that was some watering trough, but come September, Ruth and I saw Papa hitch up the wagon and head toward Shady's tub just about the time the sun had her last say. Ruth and I giggled when Papa rode past without his shirt. His sweat looked like pearls in sunlight.

"Ruth, you know our Papa looks like he is a fine specimen. Don't you think?"

Ruth never answered me at first. Then she smiled and said, "When I grow up I'm going to wear dresses like Mama with lace across my bosom."

THE WAY IT WAS
1941

It was a regular day until they found her. Black Jack and Verbenia moved on in the night, and left her right on the front porch. She wasn't even crying, just sleeping in the laundry basket Mama had given to them when the baby was born the month before.

The note, pinned on with a clothespin, said, "Better for you to have her."

So there it was, a month-old baby, pale pecan brown like Verbenia. Her name was Sadie. Mama took her in and fussed around about finding old bottles on the top shelf and getting tea towels for make-do diapers. Daddy was so upset he went off to the barn to milk, and Mama started breakfast after she moved the basket to the corner behind the stove.

"Want me to hold her, Mama," I asked, "or rock her the way Verbenia does? Want me to give her some of that bottle, or does she drink milk like that? Verbenia always nurses her. Now who's going to do that around here?" My mother had long, lean breasts, and my sister Belle didn't even have any on her yet. "What are we going to do? Send her to the orphan's place?"

"Hush, Sissy, give me some peace. I'm thinking. This is a real hard problem."

"Can't we just raise her up? Verbenia did give her to us."

"Well, this is touchy. She might be better with her own kind."

"We are her own kind."

"How many white families you know got a colored baby in the house to raise right alongside their own kids?"

About that time, the baby began to scream. Mama dropped the oatmeal ladle, picked her up, sat in the rocker, and placed the bottle to her lips. She didn't take much. The screaming lasted until she got on a dry tea-towel diaper, and Mama remembered to sing her one of Verbenia's very own songs, the one about "the Maker is a coming to set me free and turn the muddy river to sky blue."

"Can I take her to school? Bea brought her little brother when he was newborn. I could take her and show them how we got a new baby, too."

"Chastity Snow, you can't take her to school. She is not your kin."

"Yeah, she is. She's Verbenia's. I happen to love Verbenia about as much as anyone."

"Shut your mouth, girl."

My father suggested he ask Bertha to keep the baby while he tried to find Verbenia.

"Ain't never going to find Verbenia now that she's gone off with Black Jack."

"Oh, I don't know. Shiftless as he is, they'll be coming back before the well water freezes over."

"Why don't you bleach her skin with some of that lemon juice Belle puts on her freckles," I said, "if that's what you're worrying over. Un-color her skin with that lemon juice. Then she can be a regular white baby. Isn't that the problem? She can sleep in my room. In fact, she might about fit in my bottom dresser drawer if we stuff it with a blanket. Maybe Daddy can make her a bed, a birds-eye maple, like Cousin Sue's."

"Sissy, stop it. Let us think."

"I think you're making a big deal out of nothing. Daddy always brings in the baby pigs. We raise them up and no one seems to mind. We got a real live baby here, and Mama, you always said how sorry you were there weren't any more children for you. Now, see, we have one."

Baby Sadie stayed on, and when the frost turned every blade of grass in the yard to milky white, Verbenia came back. Black Jack ran off and left her, and she came home to us, thin with dark places under her eyes. Her breasts drooped like flat floursacks. The baby didn't pay her any mind, at first, just held up her arms for Mama to take her, and cried. I thought Verbenia must have felt real bad, so I held out my hands to her. She pulled me on her lap just like she used to do. I rested my head on her shoulder and felt her give a great sigh. No one mentioned the six long months she'd been gone.

The next time, Verbenia left with a man named Snake. She took Sadie with her, and Mama and I both cried. Mama said she felt sad and sorry that she's never had any more babies, and I said I was sorry not to have Verbenia any more.

Between the Lines

" I am not going!"

"Yes, you are, going now if I have to drag you all of the two miles."

"Won't go back there because I can't read the words."

"What you think your folks are sending you to school for? It's so you'll learn to read and do all those numbers, too."

"Words! I don't need to read them. You can't read. What I need reading for? I won't read in the books. I can read sky pictures and sing the bird songs. I can draw in the river-road sand."

"Road pictures don't have colors. Come on now. You said the school crayons are good for making the grass as green as alfalfa. Remember your red barn pictures? Kate, you got to go."

"No, I can learn right here, like how you make the coals light up and how the coffeepot sings. No, you can show me the catfish in the slough. Don't you know I'm best for you? School stinks. School is for others. Roy, I can come here to your place and Mama will think I'm in school."

"You're going to school. You can get some friends of your own at school."

"You're the only friend I want. Didn't you always say I was the best friend you had?"

"Well, yeah, that's true, but a girl like you needs kids to play with."

"Never had none."

"What don't you like about school?"

"Well, you got to sit all of the time, and the seats feel like fencing. Recess is good because we get a drink at the well and we run and chase each other. Nothing much happens. I mean, I don't know the letters and I don't care what happens in those book stories."

"What do you care about?"

"Why being home around you, Roy. You know, fixing things, running hogs, and going to your singings."

"What if I go to school with you?"

"You're too big. I mean, you can't fit in the seats."

"I can stand."

"All day . . . you can stand?"

"Sure, if I have to. I can go and learn to read, too."

"What for?"

"The papers, like your daddy reads, the newspapers."

"Okay, if you go to school, Roy, so will I."

Kate Stewart and Roy Wilson walked to Kin Folk Ridge School in the fall of 1942. The teacher, Miss Pratt, looked up somewhat wide-eyed when the six-foot, middle-aged colored man entered the schoolhouse.

"I am here to learn to read and write."

"I don't know. You're a grown man." Miss Pratt waved her hands in faltering movements that matched her speech.

Roy Wilson stood with his hands to his sides. Drops of sweat emerged on his forehead. "I will clean the floors and feed the fire to learn to read the same as her." Roy pointed to Kate who was looking at her teacher and twirling her fingers around her braid.

"He's my friend. Can't he stay?"

Miss Pratt nodded and pointed to a desk and chair at the back of the room. Roy smiled and moved to his designated place.

"We don't have a bigger desk," she said, "but you can get a stool from the cloakroom, one you can sit on. The chores you'll do will be those that we all help with."

The teacher handed him a pencil and a tablet which he held to his chest.

Kate took her seat, but turned often to smile at the man in the overalls. She gave him the red and green crayons when Miss Pratt left the room to hang up her coat.

The cold crept in through the edges of the steamed windows. Fingers of winter wrapped around the children's feet and twice during the morning the teacher said, "Children, stomp your feet." Roy moved his heavy boots on the oak flooring, too. He carried the coal bucket frequently to the stove in the middle of the room. He listened to the readings. The small voices wilted in the front of the room, but Miss Pratt's voice carried him to the mountains and to the sea. He sang in a baritone, "God Bless America." The children turned and stared as his voice filled the room. At midday, Miss Pratt showed Roy how to curl his callused fingers around a crimson crayon.

"Draw now," she said.

"I can't draw," he replied.

"Yes, he can," Kate offered. "He can make a picture in the river road."

Roy held the crayon close to the paper and Kate placed her hand over Roy's. Together, they moved the crayon around and around. "A flower, Roy, a flower."

Roy smiled. Kate waved his flower in the air. She carried Roy's drawing around the room. She smiled and laughed.

Miss Pratt suggested they all sing "Red River Valley" before they closed the day. Everyone helped Roy carry the ashes to be buried out back. He and Kate walked home together daily from then on until the first birds of spring returned and the stove stood empty in the classroom.

"Now, Kate, you've learned to read and can go to school without me. I'm going to be planting spring crops."

"But, Roy, you got to do it, too. I mean, read."

"Baby, I can't. In the books, the words are all a fuzz."

"The words?"

"Yeah, the words."

The next day Kate went to school alone.

"Where is Roy?" Miss Pratt asked.

"Planting. He says the words are all a fuzz, and he's not going to learn to read."

Miss Pratt's shoulders sagged. She began the day with the letters. Kate knew them all.

"Tell him I said to come on Friday, Kate."

Miss Pratt found the glasses in her uncle's store. "Are you sure?"

"Sure," her uncle said. "They'll be a start until Doc Timmons can see him."

Roy Wilson went with Kate to school on Friday, and Miss Pratt handed him the glasses. "Try them."

Roy put them on. He opened the reader and saw the clean, clear lines of the letters. He sank into a chair and traced the letters with his finger. "I can see them. How still they are! I can make a new try to read. Do you think I can?"

The teacher nodded.

Kate piped up, "See, Roy, here are all of the words we made in the sand, only littler."

"Smaller," Miss Pratt corrected.

"No, they're littler than little. In the sand we made them big with a stick."

"I know them now. They're clear as well water." Roy took the glasses off and looked at the sea of words on the paper. He put the glasses on and saw S and t and little dotted i.

"I'll be back after planting time."

"Roy, can you still see me? I mean like I am with your glasses on?"

"Sure, Kate, only now I can see you read and there's two inches taller of you. I can see you even with these glasses off. I mean, in my mind you will always be there, better than word pictures . . . friend pictures, people pictures, fluttering about in my head even on the coldest days when the weather has just kicked up a cloudburst of snow."

Kate nodded. "You know, Roy, school is nice now. And Sarah wants me to come to play on Thursday. You'll be all right. You can start to read the papers when Sarah and I play dolls. You aren't crazy about the dolls the way we are. Sarah has a dollhouse her grandpa made with real furniture. Roy, we are growing up."

Roy laughed a long laugh and began to hum something as he and Kate walked home along a road where the most incredible blue bonnets were coming open. Their blossoms were so full that they bent over on their strong stems of crayola green.

ACROSS THE RIVER

Joe was moving on. Joe. Didn't Joe belong to her? He had boiled her clothes in the yard since the day she was born, and later helped her stir the cooking laundry with his whittled walking stick.

"I'm leaving, Sue Ann," he said, "leaving for good."

She didn't believe his words. After all, her father wouldn't let Joe go nowhere. Mama said Joe was indebted to her father. Sue Ann stared up in Joe's face to see if he was joking. She poked his stomach to make him laugh, but he didn't laugh. He grabbed her hand and held on.

"Joe's really leaving. I'm going up north to pick beans and cut spinach."

"Take me, too. I don't eat much and I got a dollar saved. I can cook fried potatoes and coffee. I can work beans with you. I'm a good field hand."

"Field hand! Why you're a child, a little girl who ought not to be working for a long time. You got your dolls to sing to. I know you're going to grow to a lady, not no rough field hand."

"I can't grow up if you leave. Stay. When I'm big, I'll marry you. We'll be a family."

Joe looked away, toward the long run of cotton rows. "When you grow up, you'll marry a young man, not an old man like me.

Little girls can love in many ways, but you don't know about the world. You're like my own baby, but I'm not taking you away. You'll forget and one day understand."

"No, Joe, you stay here. You belong to me."

"A man don't belong to anyone. His heart and his soul are his own, and you can't hold a man to you by owning him."

"But I want you to stay." Sue Ann's face grew red. She kicked the old man's shins. He stood rigid and solemn. Then he grabbed the flaxen-haired child with one hand and sat her down hard on the ground.

"Listen here, you don't kick and hurt someone who loves you. You don't leave your bruises on their flesh. No knots on legs can change things. You see, Joe don't really want to stay here any longer. All of my life I wanted to see the other side of the river. If I wait any longer, I might die . . . never know nothing but cotton and hogs."

"And me, Joe, you know me. We can hide in the hay and see the owls come and go in the barn. And eggs . . . I found five laid up in the shed. Don't go. The river will swallow you."

Joe stood. He raised the child to her feet. "Go up to your house."

Sue Ann grabbed him hard around the knees and held on. He pried her loose. "Go on . . . . git!"

Sue Ann ran toward the house like a startled colt. She stopped when she saw her father fixing the rake in the yard.

"Daddy, Joe's leaving."

"Yeah, I know."

"You going to let him?"

Her father shrugged his shoulders and nodded his head. Sue Ann backed away. She turned and ran to the porch and into the house. Her mother stood at the stove.

"Joe's leaving, you know?"

"Yes, I know." She went on stirring soup, her face gone off.

Sue Ann ran from the room and up the stairs to her bedroom. She found her doll, the grown-up one in a real silk dress. She took a deep breath. The room smelled of old things. "Joe's leaving. He's not coming back. He's going to pick beans up somewhere." The doll lay still with painted lips. Sue Ann waited. Then, she shook her doll. "Don't you hear me?" The doll's dress stayed wrinkled and cool. Sue Ann pulled her doll close to her heart and rocked her back and forth.

"Bye bye baby, bye bye baby," she sang.

She cried tears enough to wet her face and the face of the doll in her arms. She dabbed her doll's eyes with her fingers.

"Now, now, you have me, pet," she said. "No more tears. You see, maybe Joe got drafted and is going off to war. When the war is over, maybe Joe will come home. Maybe he will get as far as Cottonwood Point and change his mind."

That night, Sue Ann's mama, Sarah, folded a patchwork quilt to give to Joe. Her fingers moved across the miles of tiny stitches. She hugged the quilt to her. Joe going? She would never have stayed in this mosquito-infested backdrop of civilization if Joe hadn't been around . . . Joe to fix the doors, and Joe to stew the chickens when she lay with child again and again. They were children who came and went in the night. Joe had been someone to read to and someone to cry to whenever . . .

The quilt grew heavy in her arms until Joe reached out and took it from her.

"I'm going now. You'll be fine."

In her mind Sarah said, *Joe, take me to the other side of the river.* With her lips she said, "Good-bye."

Sue Ann's father Jacob thrust money into Joe's hand, money his father had left him. He looked at the colored man before him . . . fixer of his childhood earaches, master craftsman of snake sticks, and the protector who had stood between him and his own father who wielded a razor strap when boys defied work and the land. As Joe turned to leave, for one brief moment Jacob yearned to cry out, *Joe, take me with you to the other side of the river.* Joe shifted his burden and walked down the dusty road. The moon was big enough to illuminate his path all the way to Cottonwood Point, where he waited for the ferry. The river flapped against the sunken sand. He turned and looked at his life behind him hidden in the depths of darkness.

They Laid Their Cards on the Table

Nell was the new woman who worked in the house. She was small, with dark skin, and worked in silence, but had time to smile when Martha looked her in the face. Nell finished kitchen clean-up while Martha sipped hot cocoa at the table.

"Nell, what are you going to do next? Got time to play a game of Old Maid with me?"

"No, child, I have to make the chickens ready for tomorrow."

Martha sighed and nodded. "Maybe tomorrow, or tomorrow's tomorrow?"

Nell put her coat on and went out the door. She headed toward the chicken yard. Her job was new at old man Burger's farm.

Martha swirled the last of her cocoa in her stoneware mug. She knew Nell went out to catch a young fryer or two for their Sunday dinner, and wondered if Nell would wring the chicken's neck or use the axe. Martha rinsed and dried her mug, stretched to place it in the cupboard with the others, then hung the towel on the rack by the stove.

There were sudden low sounds from the chicken yard. She stood still to listen, strained toward the noise. Suddenly she placed her hands over her ears to shelter her hearing.

"Oh, no, surely not."

Martha darted toward the door and yanked at the black knob.

She ran out into the light chill of winter. "Nell, Nell, not my chicken, not Princess."

She stopped at the paint-flaked gate in time to see Nell's arm making circles in the air. A white leghorn whirled like a Ferris wheel ride. Nell stood with her legs slightly apart while she wrung the young chicken's neck. Her arm dropped down—her hand clutched the pop-eyed chicken head, and on the ground lay a headless body. Princess did her last dance, a dance of death . . . frantic hopping movements that ended in a small flop.

Martha sent a piercing scream into the winter day. Red blotches appeared, patch-like, beneath her eyes.

"My chicken, my chicken, mine, mine, mine."

Nell's eyes widened and then covered themselves with soft brown lids. "I didn't know, child. These chickens all look alike to me. I didn't know."

Martha squatted close to the earth and ran cold fingers over her white-feathered chicken. "Princess." She looked up at Nell. "What are you crying for? You never knew Princess."

"I'm not crying for a dead chicken. I'm crying for your hurt."

Martha saw her grandfather coming across the yard. She stood up. He carried his snake stick in his wrinkled hand. His ears had long been closed to the world, but his eyes saw what he could not hear. He moved his head from left to right and then his gaze came to rest on the chicken.

"Yours?" he bellowed to the child.

Martha nodded. And then she grabbed his stick and threw it to the ground. She kicked her grandfather's legs. He didn't move. She stopped and looked at Nell, who watched with large eyes. Martha kicked her grandfather once more.

"Stop now!" he shouted.

Martha stopped and hung her head.

"Woman," the grandfather addressed Nell, "we will have salt pork for Sunday dinner. Go to the smoke house and get what you need. Go on now." He reached out and touched Nell's arm. His eyes watered. Nell walked away.

He turned to Martha. "Don't go wrapping your heart around no chicken again. Chickens are food, and there's no place for this nonsense when we have to have our table full."

Martha looked at her grandfather's face. *Help me*, she pleaded from deep inside. *Fix it.* She went to the shed to find a spade and started to dig a hole in the ground. Her grandfather looked at the plump chicken, a meal when times turn hard. Men stole for less. He lowered his shoulders, took the spade from the child, and began to dig a proper grave.

"Guess she needs some straw to rest on," he said.

Martha fetched the straw. She laid Princess in her grave.

"We can't have a real funeral cause neither one of us can sing," Martha said.

The woman Nell was back now with the salt pork under her arm. "Sing?" she said. "I can sing. Let me sing for her."

Nell hummed and strummed soft words that fell into the open grave and rested on the chicken. Martha listened and was reminded of her mother, dead now some three years. She yearned to feel her mother's arms around her. She wondered if this woman felt warm like her mother. She peeked at the singing woman. Martha wrapped her arms around herself and moved closer to Nell. She could hear Nell's voice better and felt the warm air she sent out in song.

Martha's tears began again. "Hold me. Hold me," she whispered to no one. Her grandfather didn't hear, but Nell put her hand out and pulled Martha's body into the warmth of her own.

They covered the chicken with rich soil, and the day ended under dark clouds that promised rain or maybe even snow. Martha went to bed covered with a quilt patterned in reds and yellows. Nell sang to her even though she was lost to sleep before the first note of the song arrived.

Morning came in uninvited. Martha's sleep came in stops and starts and she was reluctant to get up. Something warm moved against her back. She lay still, but turned her head to look at the moving thing. A black and white cat lay against her, not a new cat, and not a wild one born in the barn. Martha stroked the cat's head. The cat slept on, yawned, and stayed huddled into the warmth of the bed.

The bedroom door opened, and Nell spoke, "Time to be up and eat your breakfast."

"Look at this, a grown-up cat in my bed."

"Yeah, I see. You like her?"

"Oh, yes. Where did she come from?"

The woman studied the cat and said, "Guess she's been around a long time and now she's found a good home."

"Can she eat breakfast, too? Milk?"

"Now, not all cats want milk," Nell said, "but I think this cat will eat some cornbread and gravy."

The cat followed Nell to the kitchen, and Martha jumped out of bed to follow them both. The cat wound herself around Nell's legs. Nell shoved the cat toward Martha who held out a bowl of cornbread sopped in gravy. The cat darted toward the bowl. Martha laughed aloud. Her grandfather, deaf for a lifetime, turned from the breakfast table and looked at the child's face. He smiled at the woman.

Nell reached out to stroke the child's sleep-mussed hair. "I'm sure this cat has found a good home."

Martha looked at her grandfather. "Me and Nell are going to play Old Maid today, because today is yesterday's tomorrow."

The old man smiled. He heard what he saw. The room was so warm he took off his shoes and dozed while the cat washed her face clean and the child and the woman laid their cards on the table.

EASY

Wiggens was meaner than snakebite. He was the cotton foreman.

"Haul 'em up here. Lift 'em, man. Get that sack where I can hook it on these scales."

That was Wiggens hollering at the cotton pickers. He was nicer to me because I was the boss's child.

School was out for cotton picking. The whole county was off. When there wasn't cotton to work, there was spinach, tomatoes, hay or beans. I liked work in the fields better than helping Mama in the house. She was always cooking, canning, or just making ends meet.

Mama said, "Em, don't know what I'm going to do with you. Growing to be a lady and down there working in the fields, making yourself into a common sort."

I picked behind Easy. She made the row first, and I came behind her and cleaned the last bit of cotton from the bolls. Easy was colored and old and lived on the place since before Daddy was born. Some said she was a prostitute, but I didn't pay much attention to what folks said. They didn't know Easy the way I did. She knew things no book could tell you.

It was Monday morning. Easy and I were working our way down the south-forty. The sun warmed up. Sandy loam land made good cotton, river-bottom land, but sometimes the

Mississippi River sallied right up into the fields and the crop drowned. Daddy said, "That's the chance goes with farming in the bayou."

"Sleep good?" Easy asked me.

"Sure. Heard the last chapter of the Bobbsey Twins last night, and now we're going to start a new book."

"Your mama's good to read to you."

"Want me to tell you what happened?"

"No, not today. I got my mind on a mess of other things."

"What things?"

"Well, Wiggens says, 'Pick more and faster.' He says I lag and he's got a bunch of folks signed up and can't work on account of the likes of me."

"Maybe I can pick into your bag. I don't need the money much."

"No, I'll hold my own."

Easy's dark eyes glistened. She wiped the sweat from her face and turned back to her work. Her sack hung down, dragged her shoulder with it.

Wiggens . . . Wiggens, that old devil. I told Daddy how he treated the pickers, but when I did, he turned his back and shrugged and mumbled something about Wiggens being tough, honest, and a good foreman.

Wiggens got paid on how much cotton came out of the field. He had four children and a dead wife. She burned up, charred from her head to her feet.

We ate lunch under a walnut tree that grew on the edge of the field. I had egg-salad sandwiches and an apple. Easy drank coffee from her fruit jar and sucked on her pipe. Sometimes she chewed and spit. I looked the other way when she did that.

"Tell me about the river, Easy."

"I was born on the banks of the river just west of Cottonwood Point. I played on the sandbars when I was about four. One day the river sailed along at a pretty good clip and a big boat tied up. It was the Delta Queen. Never saw such a boat as that one. They played music loud enough for me to hear way before she dropped anchor. I walked closer and closer to the boat, mystified by the music, when I lost my footing and slipped right into the river. The men on the boat laughed and laughed.

"'Little dark girl fell in. Wanna fish her out? Oh, let her go, no loss anyway.'

"I thrashed and pushed and swallowed water until some hand reached out and then an arm wrapped around my belly. Man from the boat fished me out and put a blanket around me. He gave me soup and let me sit on his knee until I warmed up my scare. He weren't really no man, 'bout fifteen, I'd say. I learned after that to stay away from the river's edge. It was the music I loved. Pipe music like, made with steam and someone playing. I hummed that song a long time and made my own music by changing the ups and downs. Don't remember anyone singing that song, but I can still hum it for you."

Easy hummed, but I didn't recognize the song. I put my head on her lap and looked up into the blue sky where the clouds floated along like smoke puffs from chimneys in winter.

"Easy, do you think there's something up there besides clouds and that blue?"

She looked up for a long time. "Why sure there is. Don't you see that princess with the crown on her head? She's ready to go to a fine party with banjo strumming."

"You got that mixed up. There aren't princesses and banjo strumming."

"Who says? When you dream and make things in the sky, you don't go by the rules. Make it to suit yourself. Nothing has to be perfect or just like they tell it in one of your books."

"Oh, I know what you mean. Now let me look. I see a mountain. There's a camel climbing up with an elf on his back."

"That's it. Use your head to make your own story. Elves and camels, right interesting."

The field hands returned to the rows. Easy strained to get up. She put her hand on her back and screwed up her mouth.

"Hurting?" I asked.

"Never you mind. I'll rub it good with liniment when I get home."

Sun scorched now, burned right into my dress. I picked cotton and slid it into Easy's sack. She knew what I was doing, but she didn't say anything. She dragged her feet more and more. I heard her breathing. Wiggens, that trout, sat at the back of the truck with his feet propped up, swigging tea from a bottle.

Easy stopped and stood up stiff as a broom. She dropped her sack and moaned out loud. The top part of her body bent forward and she fell face down into the dirt. She rolled over and opened her eyes wide and gasped for air. Her skin looked a funny color. I dropped my sack and knelt beside her. Something bad was going on in her body. I stood up and screamed. Wiggens jumped off the truck and came running. The other pickers stopped work and moved closer to the heap on the ground.

Wiggens gathered her up in his arms and carried her to the truck. He put her on the truck bed. She lay limp. He patted her wrists and rubbed her arms.

"Come on, come on, Easy, don't give it up." Wiggens had turned pale. "Run child, tell your papa to come fast."

Easy was wide-eyed and honey-colored once more when Daddy and I got back to her. She held her hand on her chest and watched Wiggens. He was breathing fast and resting back on his heels.

"Sure scared me," Wiggens said. "Easy, I knew you were a tough old girl and weren't going to die on us. What you need is some rest."

Easy tried to talk, but Daddy wouldn't let her.

"Going to take you to a doctor and when you're up to it, we'll find you some work to do up at the house. This field work is too hard for you now."

Wiggens stood up. "Let's get back to work. No time to be loafing with the new bolls opening up."

Daddy touched Wiggens's arm. "Wiggens, it's been a hot one. I'm taking you off quota. Just get the most you can without working their hides off. It's a good crop, plenty for everyone. Cotton ain't worth a life."

Wiggens let out a long sigh. His shoulders sank. He nodded with understanding.

The sun dropped and the field yielded to the coming sounds of twilight. Before I could get into the truck to go home, mosquitoes were singing, on their way up from the river, and I had two fresh bites on my leg.

Encounters with Pagey

Pagey lived in a tar-papered shack on the banks of the Mississippi River in Southern Missouri. She had almond-colored skin and no wrinkles in 1943. I was seven years old. My house was a quarter of a mile down the road on my grandfather's 140-acre, river-bottom farm. I visited Pagey out of my own loneliness. There were few children for me to play with on this isolated backwoods property.

Monday was egg day. Mama sent me down to Pagey's with her week's supply of eggs. Pagey came to the sagging screen door and motioned for me to come inside. I held the sturdy egg basket up high. She relieved me of my burden with graceful hands and placed each white oval shape into a gray crockery bowl that had a chipped lip. Finished with the egg business, Pagey sat down on a cane-bottom chair. I took a seat in the only other chair in the room.

Pagey smiled and I saw her one good tooth, a gold one in the front. She waited as I concentrated on the wall behind her. Newspapers covered her walls, some yellowed from grease, smoke, and age.

I jumped up and pointed, "This one. This one."

Pagey nodded. "Yes, read that one about the ice cream social."

I stood up a little on tiptoe to get a better grasp of each

printed word. I read aloud about the fine ice cream social held on the lawn of the First Methodist Church. The newspaper article told about the ladies taking lemonade and using their fans from the funeral home to ward off the heat. I finished a lengthy description, and Pagey sighed and smiled. We liked to share the old newspaper stories. Pagey said it brought life inside her house. I likened it to the books lined on the shelves of the library uptown in Caruthersville.

"Child, want to make some fried potatoes?"

I nodded. Mama never let me cook at home. She said I was too young and got in her way. Pagey seemed to have a lot of time to do the things I liked.

Pagey poured some well water into an enamel pan in front of me. She placed two rather dirty potatoes by the water. I washed each one and laid them aside to dry. Pagey placed a gob of grease in a skillet on the small wood stove. I peeled the potatoes and Pagey sliced them.

"I never get potatoes that taste like these at home."

"Well, cooking needs love to make it come out right."

The potatoes fried in bacon fat until browned and good. The smell was the best part. I ate my potatoes and licked the last of the greasy goodness from my fingers.

Sometimes Pagey got a letter and Mama sent me down the road with it. On Tuesday, a large white envelope came with Pagey's name printed across the front. Entrusted with the letter, I walked the sandy quarter of a mile to make my delivery. Pagey opened the door and I eagerly pressed the large envelope toward her. She took the envelope with hesitation and placed it on a table. I wondered when she was going to ask me to read the letter for her.

"I guess I'd better get on with reading your letter because Mama needs me to pick strawberries."

I wondered who in the world would write to Pagey. No one

ever even came along the road to ask about her. I opened the letter, easy like. Pagey nodded approval of the way I handled her letter. I read in a loud voice.

Dear Miss Pagey Smith:
    I am sorry to tell you that your father, Lawson Smith, passed away. Burial: Carson's landing on the 23 of June. We did not know how to contact you any sooner. We extend sympathy to you in your loss. Lawson Smith was a good man, a hard worker, and a friend in the deepest sense of the word. My wife and I will sadly miss him.
Sincerely,
John Owens

That was all. There were no more words for me to hide behind. I looked down at the paper before me, and Pagey didn't move. She folded her hands on her lap. I reached out and laid my hand atop her beautiful ones. Her eyes looked moist and frightened.

"My father was old. He has passed. I am fixing to get ready to go to his funeral now. Run on home."

I nodded and ran out of the door and down the hot river-road afraid of my sadness for my friend. I didn't want to feel this hurt, but it was holding on inside of me. Pagey's hurt.

Pagey went away for her father's funeral. She wore a small hat and a dark dress which clung to her thin body. When the hired man drove her home again, I ran behind his dust cloud to greet her at her door.

"Mama sent you this sponge cake." I unwrapped it on her table and sat down to share its golden goodness. We finished our cake as the bob white's call reminded us that evening was coming.

"Pagey, I don't mind if you cry about your father's passing. It would make me feel a lot less sad. I know I'm going to cry a whole lot when you die. Is that all right with you?"

"Positively all right, child, and thank you for caring."

Pagey smiled at me through the screen door. "Come tomorrow, and we'll make biscuits for lunch. My father's preacher sent some sorghum."

I left her with biscuits and dying in my thoughts.

The biscuits rose up light and tasted good with the sorghum. After lunch, I read two newspaper clippings from the wall behind the bed; one told about a president's duties and the other about the work that they did in the war plants. Pagey said, "President Roosevelt is a good President." I didn't really know, but I agreed with her.

As I left the house, I caught and ripped my dress on the rough part of the door. Pagey said, "Wait, I'll mend it for you."

I slipped off my dress and waited in my petticoat while Pagey sewed. She made tiny stitches.

"Oh, I wish I could do that," I sighed.

"Bring along some material tomorrow," Pagey said.

The next day I found a piece of printed material left over from one of Mama's dresses and took it for my first sewing lesson at Pagey's.

"Can I make a dress?"

"No, start with something easier," she suggested.

"All right, I'll make an apron for you."

We spent several days sewing on the apron. When the task was finished, Pagey put it right on and started cooking.

I sewed many things after that, with Pagey humming along beside me. She shelled peas or rocked herself into a light slumber.

I told Pagey about my school and some of the things we learned. She listened and asked a lot of questions. Sometimes I'd take along a pad and pencil and she began to practice to make letters for herself. Her hands shook as she moved through the alphabet. I tried not to look too closely at her efforts. One day when I arrived, she showed me a paper on the table. I read what she had written in her shaky script: "Miss Pagey Smith." She drew her willowy frame up tall and we shared her moment of pride in silence.

My cooking and sewing improved. Pagey's writing got better. By fall, I had read almost every newspaper story on her walls. Then I brought my father's recent newspapers to read about the happenings of the present day. My reading was slow. Sometimes I didn't know the words and together we guessed at the meaning. Pagey began to identify words for herself and read my reader that year. We never talked about her reading and writing. It just happened to us.

My father moved us to a town some ninety-five miles away from my grandfather's farm in 1946. My encounters with Pagey ended. She died in 1956. Her passing went unnoticed by me until I visited my grandparents' farm and asked about her. She had been dead for several months. My grandmother gave me a box with my name on top in Pagey's shaky script.

Inside the box I found our practice-writing sheets, scraps of material, a large white envelope announcing the passing of Lawson Smith, and newspaper clippings from 1946. My tears ran as I remembered days of biscuits and dying.

"Pagey . . . Pagey . . . lovely almond-skinned woman, I've cried for you. This blond-haired child, turned woman, kept her promise to cry at your passing.

Amalgamation Cake

Emma Baker and Bessie Walker lived two miles apart, in the country, six miles from town on farms where they each tended a garden, raised their own laying hens, and managed households with four children apiece. Emma was content with her lot in life, except for one annoying problem that festered every Christmas holiday season. Bessie Walker refused to give Emma her Amalgamation Cake recipe.

"No, Emma, I'm not-a-gonna do it! This cake has been in my family for generations and no one is going to have the recipe. You'll have to be content with me giving you and yours one ready-made cake to grace your table every Christmas. That's enough for any one God-fearing woman to expect from another."

So there it was—year after year the Baker family ate Bessie Walker's one gift cake with its luscious goodness only at Christmas time, and alas, it was heard tell the Walkers kept a generous supply of the heavenly delicacy in their pantry, behind their cook stove, all winter long.

When the children grew tall enough, and old enough, to ride together to town on one of the Bakers' mares, a terrible tragedy occurred right before Christmas. Emma was alerted to the situation when she heard her phone sound out two longs and one short. She knew that was the sheriff's ring.

Amalgamation Cake

She picked up the receiver to listen in and recognized her dear friend Bessie Walker's voice. She sounded loud and irritated.

"That's right, Sheriff Cooper, my entire brood of chickens is gone, even the rooster. That pack of wild dogs sucked every egg in the hen house and left my chickens dead. You have to do something!"

"Well, Mrs. Walker, you know as well as I do, might have been a coyote's party or a fox's ambush. Can't do much about that."

"What about my Amalgamation Cake?"

So there it was. Emma Baker put the receiver back on the telephone. What about Bessie's cake? What in the world was Bessie stewing around about her cake when her chickens were gone? That was it . . . her egg supply was gone. Emma was beginning to understand when her telephone's ring came on . . . two longs.

"Hello? Why Bessie, I was just thinking about you! What? You want to buy twenty-four eggs from me? Gracious, I don't know. They haven't been laying good and with Christmas coming on—I don't know. What you need all that many eggs right now for?"

Silence sailed past with a breeze that promised the falling of new pecans from the tree out back.

Bessie Walker's voice came across the wire, calmer and softer. "Emma, you see to it I get two dozen eggs as often as your hens lay them, and I will see to it you have my recipe."

"Mercy me, Bessie Walker, this is going to be the nicest Christmas present you ever gave me."

And that Christmas in 1923 two farm women cemented their life-long friendship by sharing a cake that combined foods from their daily lives—AMALGAMATION CAKE!

AMALGAMATION CAKE RECIPE

2 ½ cups sugar
2 cups butter
1 cup buttermilk
4 cups flour
¾ cups white raisins
10 eggs, beaten separately
¾ cups pecans
3 t baking soda
1 t cinnamon
1 t allspice
1 ¼ pts. strawberry jam

Cream butter and sugar. Add beaten egg yolks. Add jam. Add flour, spices, and soda that have been sifted together. Fold in beaten egg whites.

Bake in layer pans lined with waxed paper, 45 minutes at 300 degrees. Makes two layer cakes.

Put together with following filling:
2 ½ cups sugar
1 heaping cup white raisins
1 cup sweet milk
14 egg yolks
1 cup butter

Cook filling in double boiler until thick. Remove from fire. Add 2 cups nuts, 2 cups ground coconut or canned coconut, and 2 t vanilla.

A Long Time Ago

My friend Sheila thought she was smart, pretty, and rich. She was. We were seven and seat-mates at the Kin Folk Ridge School. I loved Sheila. I also hated her. She was always bragging around about her pony, her papa, and her Sunday school. I wanted to brag, too, but bragging takes a lot of practice.

"Sheila," I said, "My sister had rickets and I had chickenpox and measles."

She sneered her snippy face all over the place.

One Sunday I was listening to the radio, not really listening, mostly thinking about what to do about Sheila. I'd been to Sunday school and still had on my taffeta. Taffeta was good for rustling when you walked around, but my taffeta was Cousin Sarah's first and there wasn't a rustle left in that dress. It was limp and all worn out of rustle and shine. There was a hole in the material under the arm, a finger-poking hole. I kept my arms down at Sunday school so the kids wouldn't see it. They weren't looking anyway. My Cousin Sarah was there in her new rabbit coat and all of those dumb kids stood around pawing that fur to death. We had a lot of rabbits on the farm. Who needs a rabbit coat? Fur is definitely for rabbits.

"Em, get up and change your Sunday dress, right now."

Ma was hollering. What did she think could possibly happen

to my dress with me sitting and thinking in the front room? Someday I planned to wear the tail right out of that dress, dig a hole and bury it. The fuss Ma made over a used up dress!

I changed clothes quickly.

"Ma, there's new people moved in down the road. Can I go visit? They have a mess of kids, and they're going to go to my school."

"I don't know. They're probably poor white trash."

"There's no one around here to play with. Please, can I?"

I knew they wouldn't be anything like Sheila. She lived in a mansion on a plantation, said she was upper crust. Ma said we were poor, but decent people. I wondered what decent meant. I knew about poor.

Ma let me go. I promised not to stay long. When I got there, they were all inside. I knocked until the door opened. Lots of faces stared out at me. My feet felt tired. I shifted my weight and said, "I'm Em."

They all looked until the ma came to the door. Her jaws sucked in and lines were drawn right into her face.

"What is it?" she said.

"I'm Em, live down the road. Can I come in?"

We all stood around looking at each other, once I was inside. I began to feel like one of those movie people featured at the Rogers' show on Saturdays. The kids looked and looked at me until the ma brought a chair and pointed for me to sit down. I sat, and then it happened. I started all this bragging.

"We got some sows and lots of little pigs. My pa says that's bacon and money in the bank. I go to the Methodist church, know 'Jesus Loves Me' real good. My sister can read, but Papa said he's going to whip her if she reads *God's Little Acre* any more."

The room swelled with people, thin, bone-poking people. No one had very good clothes on and the baby wore a tea-towel diaper. Dirt streaked his cheeks. Tears washed a road right down his face.

I kept on bragging. My voice took on this high tone. "My pa is going to plant grass and Ma won't be sweeping the yard again."

I counted eight kids in the family. Maybe they could play Red Rover Red Rover like during recess at school. Except I never played at recess. I watched mostly to see how Sheila ran in her patent-leather shoes. Maybe these kids could play Red Rover with me.

The ma smiled. "Supper's ready. You stay and eat with us."

I looked around. Everyone waited. I stood up, and in my best voice I said, "I'd be proud to."

I sat by a girl called Ruth. I ate the biggest pie-tin of fried potatoes I'd ever eaten. *Ruth, a Bible name,* I thought. I looked at her and she looked at me.

"Will you be my friend?" she said.

She had stringy hair and wore a faded dress. Her eyes were big with spots of sad. And then, she smiled. I smiled back and nodded my head.

I asked for more potatoes. The ma looked at me and said, "We're glad you're here."

BILLIE JEAN

Billie Jean's auburn hair curled in a whimsical way and framed her heart-shaped face. That wasn't too much to mind, auburn hair that curled and green eyes. My hair was straight and yellow. The part I could hardly stand was the pony. She had a pony of her own and rode him to school every day, seated on a slick black saddle with golden tassels. Her English-style riding boots barely touched the stirrups. She was a pro when it came to riding Peppy. She walked him nice and easy at first, but sometimes she'd dig her heels into his flanks to encourage speed. Back and forth they flew, a gallop ahead of a parade of dust balls. We kids huddled together and became comrades of silent longing and admiration.

What I wanted more than anything was for Billie Jean to like me, to be my special friend, but I didn't know her much. I didn't know anyone much. My mother said I was shy. I wasn't really. I was scared, scared I'd make a mistake or get the answer wrong. Billie Jean knew all of the answers, and she made 100s all day long. Gold stars covered her notebook. She was the number-one speller in our whole eight grades and got to help primers read their lessons in circle. When Billie Jean swung at recess, we could see her petticoats, all roses and lace. I held my dress down tight between my legs when my swing went high. My slip was holes in one part, my sister's before me.

And then it happened. The teacher, Miss Leslie, paired Billie Jean and me for the nature report. We had to catch twenty-five insects, mount them, and label them. Billie Jean turned her rosebud mouth down when she heard the assignment. Wide-eyed and bewildered, she glanced toward me. "I know how to get some grand bugs," she whispered. "Can you come over to my house Saturday?"

"Sure," I said, imagining a whole day of pony rides.

Saturday at one o'clock, my mother drove me in our old Chevrolet to Billie Jean's house.

"Now Em, mind your manners," my mother began. "They say Billie Jean's mother is sickly, but her daddy's real nice. He goes to church at the Ridge."

"Wish Daddy would have washed the car before we left. It looks like some old trash heap."

"Well, Em, they aren't caring about our car. You're the part they care for. You look fine. You look grown-up for ten."

Billie Jean was waiting on the porch when we got there. She ran right out to the car and helped me carry the butterfly nets and bug bottles. She was wearing jodhpurs and boots.

"Hope you don't mind catching most of the bugs, Em. I can't kill those little things."

"Remember, Billie Jean, this is in the name of science. Hey, look, there's a Monarch butterfly circling the roses."

We hurried to the end of the garden where the roses clung to the fence. One lone butterfly perched on a flower. I brought the net down and captured our first specimen for the project.

"Are you going to kill it?" Billie Jean asked.

"Yeah, I have to. See this fruit jar? There's a cotton ball in the bottom, soaked with chloroform."

Billie Jean's's green eyes misted up.

"Tell you what," I said, "you look over there and I'll put the butterfly to sleep in the bottle. It's not bad. Not like people."

This was going to be a long day. I searched for the stable, remembered the pony, but there were lots of buildings and they all looked alike. "Where's your pony?"

She jerked her thumb toward a distant building.

"Can I ride him later?"

Billie Jean nodded her head yes. She settled down on a large rock while I went on to catch bugs. I was so busy with my work that I never saw or heard Billie Jean's mother until she was close behind me. I turned around to show Billie Jean a daddy long-legs. A woman blocked the path. Her red hair hung down to her knees, straight and limp. Her clothing clung to her thin body, and she was barefoot. She looked poor, not like Billie Jean at all. I saw the strangest sight on her wrist—an honest-to-goodness Mickey Mouse watch!

"Ma, go on back in now." Billie Jean said, "This is my school friend. Go."

The woman turned. Her eyes grew larger. I sank smaller into my shoes when she looked at me. This woman before me was somewhere outside of herself. A trickle of sweat rolled down my neck and under my dress. Defying my fear, I moved one step forward and held out my hand. "Pleased to meet you."

"What you got, girl?" She pointed toward my cigar box.

"Specimens for science."

"Let me see."

She came closer. "This here's a Monarch butterfly," I said. "She's one of the loveliest creatures in the meadow."

"Is she dead?"

"No, only sleeping," I lied.

I opened the box with care. Beneath a layer of daisies I had added, the Monarch was mounted with pins.

Billie Jean's mother sank onto a rock. She looked at the butterfly for a long time. "Did you capture this beauty, girl?"

"Yes," I whispered.

"Creature beauty is best, don't you think?"

The woman looked more real, not so wild now. Billie Jean moved closer to us and in a soft voice she said, "Ma, go in the house."

"It's okay, Billie Jean. She wants to understand."

"She'll understand you with a whip."

Her mother picked two daisies and walked toward the house. Her feet barely touched the path, and the only thing I heard was Billie Jean crying.

"Are you going to tell about her?" she asked.

"No, I won't talk about your ma. She ain't right, is she?"

Billie Jean shook her head from side to side, and at the same time she dug her finely oiled boot into the clover that clung to the dry soil. Her auburn curls drew up in the heat and her freckles stood out.

"Want to see me ride my pony? These old bugs bore me."

I turned to look once more at the Monarch. I touched the velvet wings. "I'm sorry, really sorry."

"Come on, Em, I'm going to saddle up Peppy."

My attention sharpened. After all, my greatest desire was to ride the pony. I noticed something wild and glowing flicker in Billie Jean's eyes as she turned and ran toward the distant buildings.

In what seemed like a very long time, Billie Jean appeared, leading the wonderful pony. He wore a bright red plume in his bridle. She led him to a block of wood which she stepped on to elevate herself one foot to the stirrups. Moving into the saddle, she turned and smiled at me. She clasped the reins against Peppy's neck, and they rode off. Billie Jean galloped her pony back and forth with her back straight and her head high. Her auburn hair glistened in the breeze as they raced past me again and again.

I waited. I wet my lips and cleared my throat. My fingers found coolness in my palms. I swallowed often as I shielded my eyes from the falling sun. I rehearsed in my mind the procedure for mounting the pony and holding the reins with just the right tension. My heart knew the quivering thrill that would be mine to ride in the wind with the sun on my back. But the sun drooped, and there was no mistake that my family car was coming up the road. It was time to go. I was going to have to leave. It had to be my turn now that my mother was coming to pick me up, but Billie Jean, on seeing the car, turned Peppy toward the sun and galloped further away. She waved once.

I stood bolted to the road by my disappointment until my mother's voice startled me. "Em, get in!"

I slammed our car door without looking at my mother.

"Have fun?"

"Yeah, but pony riding isn't as much fun as I thought it would be."

My mother patted my knee. I looked at her dark hair and gray eyes. She wore her second-best dress, the blue one with the flowers. I slid over by her and laid my head on her cool shoulder. I smelled her perfume. It was Blue Waltz.

"Pony riding isn't much, Mama, and did you know I am never ever going to catch another Monarch butterfly, not even in the name of science."

Snakeskin Shoe Outlet

Velda watched the clock. In twenty minutes she could close the store. Tonight, Christmas Eve, all the stores in town closed early, but not the Harley Snakeskin Shoe Outlet. No, old man Harley kept this place on schedule no matter what day it was. Velda wanted to get home and finish her packing for her trip to her sister's for Christmas. She was glad she'd cashed her paycheck on her noon hour and paid all of her bills. She still had the ten-dollar bill. Velda patted her dress pocket, thankful for her bus-fare money, enough to get to her sister's. For once, she wasn't going to spend Christmas alone.

She hummed "Silent Night" all the way down aisles A and B while she straightened the shoes. The hand on the clock pointed to five minutes until six, but there was no mistaking the tinkle of the bell over the store's front door. Winter air rushed up aisle B before the door closed. Velda moved toward the front of the store.

There they were . . . two kids standing on the rubber door-mat.

"Kids, don't y'all know this store closes in five minutes? Better get on home now."

The girl shook her dark red curls back and forth and pressed her lips forward. She looked to be about seven. The boy spoke in a gruff voice. "We gotta get our mother a present. She wants

77

some snakeskin shoes for dancing . . . red ones."

Velda frowned at the kids. They wore thin tennis shoes with the logos peeled off. The girl's coat was one of those pink, fleecy, K-Mart specials, but her coat's fleece looked like a fresh-sheared lamb. The boy had red ears and no hat.

"Shoes? Maybe you'd better let your momma come in and get them. You know, so she can try them on for size."

"No need," the girl pleaded from dark eyes. "She wears size six. I saw the size on her shoes at home. We got money."

Velda hated to ask, "How much?"

The boy was down aisle C. The girl followed. He set out a pair of sandals decorated with Christmas glitter, a pair of red pumps, and an assortment of other styles. The girl squatted to examine each pair. She ran her hand over the pattern of each shoe, a practiced eye searched for flaws.

Velda failed to hear old man Harley's key turn in the back door.

"What's this? It's five past six and you haven't locked up? What are these kids doing? Playing with the shoes?"

"No sir, they're shopping for their momma's Christmas shoes."

"With what?"

"Never you mind, Mr. Harley. I'm holding their money for them right here in my pocket while they choose." Velda had a sinking feeling when she heard what she had said. The runny-nosed boy moved quickly. He thrust his sister's hair aside and whispered in her ear. She nodded. Velda knew it was a done deal.

The girl held up the red pumps in one hand and two crumpled dollar bills in the other. Mr. Harley stood with his back to the children while he looked out of the store's front window.

"Snowing good now. You notice how like magic it comes right on time to give us another blessed Christmas."

Velda took the ten-dollar bill from her pocket, smoothed it out on the counter before putting it into the register and ringing up the sale. She stuffed the two crumpled damp bills from the girl into the toe of one red shoe. She was surprised to see the girl's fawn-like eyes watching her. Small lights flickered there. The children moved to the door with their package. She heard them leave. Through the smile on her lips, she said, "Merry Christmas!"

From somewhere deep inside she heard, *Blessed are the little children.* Next to that thought came a sinking moment. Mr. Harley left when Velda turned out the lights in the store. The snow shone so brightly through the window she didn't need any light to see the wrapped package on the counter. The card said:

For My Dearest Worker
Velda
From Mr. Harley

Velda stared long and hard at the word, "Dearest." Underneath the package she found a crisp new twenty-dollar bill. At the end of the counter she found a nickel red sucker wrapped in crumpled paper, decorated with stickers and tied with a damp green ribbon.

THE KINDEST COVER

Snow sifted over the farm like fine white flour from a gray Missouri sky. The woodpile clung to itself in the shed where logs seasoned and dried. Joel and Heather gathered the wood and trudged across the back stretch of yard. The snow softened the patch which twisted between family tombstone arches. They were all there, Heather's mother and father, her grandparents. In the past three years, smaller stones had been added for her babies, children that came and went in the night like delicate snowflakes that never touched the ground.

Heather hurried to catch up with her husband.

"Joel, wait. Come kiss me under the mistletoe." Heather was walking in an area where the mistletoe climbed and twisted overhead. That was when she spotted the fawn. "Looks like we have a lost deer."

Joel put the wood by the back door. "Heather, come on. Its mother is probably waiting for you to get out of the way."

"No, Joel, this one is alone."

"You know the rule—no creatures from the woods. Come on."

Heather stopped and squatted close to the ground, but the fawn startled and sprinted into the black grove of trees. Somewhere in the distance a single gunshot channeled into the stark, still morning. Heather went to the house where Joel worked to start a fire in their one-hundred-year-old fireplace. She rubbed moisture from the beveled windowpane and was surprised to see the fawn again, right under the arch of the mistletoe.

"Joel, the fawn is back. She has no mother. I know it."

"So leave it be. Let nature take its course."

His words stung, like a slap against the cold of her cheeks. *Nature's course was not always fair or right.*

Heather went to the kitchen to put on the tea. She placed biscuits and blackberry jam for Joel on a stoneware plate, and went to the barn with her softest steps to fill one of her mother's pie tins with bits of lespedeza. It still carried the aroma of hay fields in summer.

After Joel finished his tea, he fell asleep in her father's rocking chair by the fire. She heated goat's milk and placed it outside by the first offering of food. The day passed, but the food lay untouched.

In the evening, Joel chopped a hole through the ice in the horse trough, and the young fawn appeared at the end of the path, posed like a yard statue frozen in time. Heather approached her again. This time she saw that the fawn was not alone. There was another one, a matched pair, no taller than her twin babies' headstones. She inched her way down the path and the fawns paused.

"Come now, here's milk to make you strong," but the fawns flitted away, this time going even deeper into the dark grove of trees. The warm, pale milk dribbled from the bottle's nipple onto the snow-crusted ground. She didn't hear Joel behind her until he spoke.

"Do you want them? What about when we get them herded into the barn and you get them eating and living off of us?"

"A little while, Joel, and then they can go right back into the woods. I can be their mother for a few weeks."

Heather knew Joel. He would find a way to bring them to

her.

The first fawn came out into the open later that night. Joel brought her, wrapped in his mother's wedding-ring quilt, in by the fire. He held his arms around her, and she eagerly accepted the goat's milk with wide-open brown eyes. The second fawn lay too still, and Heather felt a small shudder of fear when Joel carried her in. She wouldn't drink and died before dawn.

Within a few weeks, the surviving fawn ate an array of vegetarian fare, including the vines that graced the walls of the barn. On December 24th she pranced out the open barnyard gate and toward the distant wooded area at the top of a hill. She stood still for a moment before she disappeared into the tapestry of cottonwoods. And Heather knew that this one, this wild fawn, was a survivor.

.

RED FLANNEL CIRCLE

On Christmas morning, Nathan Nakowski watched his wife Eileen polish her reflected image in their breakfast teakettle with great circular motions and cloth cut from one of their son Arthur's flannel shirts. Eileen appeared as lost to her work as Nathan was to her repetitive movement. Each searched for a place to stop, but like a rolling ball had to go on until momentum rolled out.

"Eileen, sit with me. Have your tea and biscuit before you start to clean. Be still for Christmas."

The woman turned from the fire. Her eyes were shadow circles above her dress which was starched as crisp as Missouri's blue sky. Nathan looked out the window, where cold hovered above the winter ground, and then back to his wife who wore a flushed girl's face for a moment, one he remembered but seldom saw.

Eileen folded the red flannel rag, placed it on the table between them, that patch of their son's shirt, taken from one he left behind when he went away as silently as a dewdrop at dawn. Nathan had watched her cut off first the sleeves for dusting the stair banister, and then the front right side of the shirt for scrubbing the entry hall, and then the left shirt panel, the part that Arthur had worn over his heart, the square that now lay folded between them.

Nathan reached across the table, touched the tips of Eileen's plump fingers one by one, and drew around her hand with his index finger. She did not move. He stopped and took up the red flannel cloth she had folded. Like a parent, he unfolded the square, smoothed it out on the table, and placed the scrap of cloth over his wife's rough hand. He felt her hand, warm beneath his own, relax under the remnant that was once Arthur's flannel shirt.

"Eileen, for every loss, there is . . ." but his voice left him to clear his throat and he watched the fire fan itself into a few coals. Nathan pulled on boots and buttoned his coat to go out and haul in wood.

Snow dusted the stilted cornstalks in the garden and a boulder of ice rose from the horse trough. The lean-to woodshed stood next to the barn where ash and cottonwood logs held fortress against the wall of winter that surrounded the farm. The logs clanked and bounced against the earthen floor as Nathan sorted and tossed enough wood to stay the fire for the day and night. Arthur's old Rosebud Flyer sled hung high on a hook by the woodshed door. Nathan lifted it with one hand and stacked his wood on the pale red sled. That was when he noticed a gunnysack slumped in the corner with the strange dog. He squatted, stilled his own breathing, and stared. A waif of a dog lay curled into himself, brown fur matted, caked with dirt and dry blood.

"Here, now. Come."

The dog shuddered, emitted a low, rolling cry, and thumped his tail three times against the ground.

"It's okay. Let me take a look at you."

The dog skittered to stand on three legs. His right front paw was gone. Left trapped in the woods?

"Come."

But the animal lay grounded in fear. Nathan looked up. Eileen stood at the woodshed door. She stared at the dog. The dog watched.

"Get some kerosene. Let's tie up his stump."

Eileen returned with kerosene and strips of white rags. She cleansed the dog's wound with long strokes while Nathan's hand held the dog's jaws closed. He remained still against Nathan who could still smell wet soil trapped in damp fur. After the wound was clean, Eileen took out the one remaining strip of Arthur's shirt, the yoke that had covered his back, something their son outgrew, didn't need when he went away. She tore the red flannel into wide bands and wound it around the wounded appendage. Nathan lifted the animal and Eileen opened her arms.

He heard her voice scold the cold and the ways of the world, a conversation in solo as she carried the dog toward the house. "You are going to learn to make do with three legs. This I promise you."

The animal's body yielded to her swaying walk through new snow, nestled into her rhythm, and while they walked, the winds stirred the firs and Nathan heard their own Hallelujah because it was Christmas, and because a new year lay before them.

A Bus to Memphis

The Lord only knows she never meant to leave, but the heat and the smell of the hogs was overbearing. Seemed the only way was to catch the Greyhound bus and get on down to Memphis. Anna Grace always wanted to go and see something more than poor folks toting cotton from their places on a share basis and raising leghorns and pigs.

Jeremiah would raise up the devil when he found her gone, but he'd manage with the babies soon as his temper cooled and he had time to heal his aches with mudpacks from the river. He loved that river, especially the little bib-shaped beaches that reached halfway to Tennessee when the water lay low. Hadn't she put those mudpacks on his naked body just last summer to soothe his angry muscles, sore from work? Quiet he got, like some baby, all sprawled out on the beach, naked as a jay, with the mud and rushing water.

Jeremiah would do just fine with the boys. She, herself, would feel the most strung out inside, but didn't she have the right to go to Memphis and see the stores and hotels?

She smoothed her dress down across her stomach and checked to see if her good shoes looked clean. Mama Hayden sewed up this dress from the finest chambray, and all of the gathers in the skirt fell soft and gentle across her hips. She fingered her pearls, just once, and checked the waves in her hair, ironed in with care. Never mind the pangs of wrongdoings over running off. Someday, she'd come back. Someday, she'd be ready to be somebody's wife and mother, but today, well today, it was Memphis, and maybe a job in a store. Anna Grace pulled her legs up under her and rested her head against the cool glass of the bus window.

"Lord, help and guide me," she whispered to herself. "I'm not a bad girl, just a free soul searching for a light to carry that doesn't go with chopping cotton and boiling diapers outside."

Somewhere about half-way to Memphis . . . somewhere in the lands of Arkansas, he got on. Anna Grace awakened from a light sleep in time to see him board and swing his bag overhead.

"Seat taken?" he asked.

She shook her head as he claimed the seat beside her. His hair was black as a Berkshire hog and lay close to his head. Anna Grace looked away but there was nothing to see. Night pitched in the window like a spare blanket on a bed. The bus rushed on, hounding the dark curves of Highway 61 like someone's best dog. The stranger leaned back, but his limbs fell out and onto her side of the seat. She felt his arm against hers, and his knees jostled against her own with familiarity each time the bus dipped in the dark. She was startled, at first, and then her body longed to know more of his sweet warmth which spilled out in the night. He snored. She leaned back and never moved his head resting close to her shoulder. His breathing slowed and lingered. His snoring stopped, but the scent of him, tobacco and fresh alfalfa, brought Anna Grace thoughts of new mowed hay. Jeremiah would need her help. Sweet . . . sweet hay. Stop! She must stop. The man awakened. He straightened up his body and moved into his own space.

"Sorry. Did I crowd you?"

"Some."

"Going to Memphis?"

"Yeah. You?"

"I'm going to get a job."

"No work here? Girl, you are too pretty to be by yourself. You got a man?"

Anna Grace turned away. She was not able to out and out lie to the stranger. "I'm married. Got some kids."

"Must be a crazy man to let you go."

"No. Maybe I'm crazy to leave."

The stranger fell silent. Arkansas crept by and the night lingered in smoke and occasional lights.

Anna Grace let her body relax. Sleep came down and closed her eyes.

This time the stranger felt the pressure of her warm arm against him. Her head became a wobbling rag doll's until he steadied it against his shoulder. He longed to press the young woman to him . . . to stop the bus and take her out and across the field of Arkansas where he would lay her down in his early life in a cabin. He could almost hear his babies calling in the heat of the summer. But his wife . . . hadn't she left him? He didn't hunt her or beg her to come home. His pride built walls around him, and he raised his kids and let her go. He shuddered in the dark. The young woman beside him murmured, "Jeremiah." He put his arm around her as the night darted by. She slept long and hard and his lips, ever so slightly, grazed her brow when the bus dipped again.

Memphis and morning came. Anna Grace was surprised to find her comfortable place, resting on the shoulder of the stranger.

"Here she is. Memphis. Want to have a bite to eat with me?"

She nodded.

"You know, I been thinking. I might show you all about Memphis and then, about five o'clock, I could put you on the bus going back to the Bootheel. Girl, you can't stay down here long, 'cause somebody up there in Missouri loves you."

Anna Grace listened.

"Someone named Jeremiah needs you, baby, unless you want to make music with an old soul like me."

She looked at the stranger and held out her hand. "We'll see about that," she said.

They left the bus and walked a short distance to The Honey Dripper Cafe to order breakfast before Memphis even knew they were there.

A Family Gathering

Hazelwood, her former husband, was taking their two teenage daughters to the Cayman Islands for Christmas, and she was having her family for the traditional dinner and gift exchange. In her heart she knew that wasn't what she wanted. She envisioned herself on the beach with her daughters who came home infrequently between college semesters. Somehow, the idea of preparing pumpkin pies from sugar-free recipes, and low-fat everything for her daddy's increased cholesterol, Uncle Harold's blood sugar, and her mother's newly acquired dwindling appetite reminded her of her inability to relax and enjoy holidays the way she once did. She could hear her mother.

"Libby, I don't have any appetite. Nothing tastes good, not the way it used to."

She wished she had her mother's disinterest in food. Since the divorce, she found herself focused on food, making endless trips to the refrigerator. The old refrigerator lasted as long as their marriage, twenty years. The new one was short, with an intrusive hum and an interior light that shone like a headlight across the kitchen floor.

The phone rang. She hurried to pick up the receiver. Her mother's voice sounded thin, far off, even though she lived a mere two miles away.

"Libby, is everything set for dinner? We'll bring Uncle Harold.

A Family Gathering

There's this poor bachelor named Isaac something or another lives in a flat upstairs over Harold's. He doesn't have a stick of family. I didn't think you'd mind. I invited him to Christmas dinner. With your father and me, Uncle Harold, Aunt Peg and her Robby, you, and now Isaac, that's seven. You have my Haviland service for twelve, but with both girls gone . . ." Her mother's voice trailed off as though she had walked into another room.

"Isaac's fine, Mama, but no more." She knew her mother meant well. A sudden impulse forced her to add, "Does Isaac have special food considerations?"

"He doesn't eat red meat. He prefers fish, but don't worry, I'm bringing a fish casserole for him. Salmon. That's the fish clears out your arteries."

"Mama, nobody does fish casserole. This is Christmas. Can he eat a little turkey?"

"No! The man eats fish. Show respect. Who ever said you had to eat turkey on Christmas? It's important to go that extra when guests have different traditions. Don't forget, don't add extra salt. I'll give you my recipe for dressing. I'll do pies."

"What's Aunt Peg bringing?"

"Oh, I told her not to bother. She has problems with her cataracts. And her hearing is worse."

"Mama, since when does a person's hearing have a thing to do with cooking?" And then she surprised herself by saying, "Someone's at the back door." She only wished someone was. The nodding limbs of the ash drummed in the wind, demanded she come out. She opened the door and stood on the porch, examined the length of her yard, and opened her mouth to taste the bite in the wind. She cradled her body in both her arms and looked into the eye of winter, all around her, holding, waiting, and alone.

When she returned to the kitchen, the heat turned her thoughts to her daughters, Holly and Anne, and their trip with their father. It felt like it was always his time to have them. She didn't want them not to go. What she wanted was to go, too. Tomorrow was Wednesday and she would do much holiday cooking ahead of time.

Isaac. What did her mother say his last name was? Uncle Harold was in his late seventies, so she supposed Isaac was of his generation.

Holly and Anne drove in from college on Wednesday and packed what looked like a dismal array of wrinkled tops and shorts. Their bikinis didn't take up much room, and they decided to take just one dress. The ocean breezes of Libby's mind fanned the kitchen and steamed the windows as she sliced carrots.

"Mom, aren't you doing something with your hair before your big dinner tomorrow? It's ragged. Glo's mom has this long braid, and when she goes out, she wraps it around the back of her head in an S shape. It gives her height. Maybe you could grow yours out."

"By tomorrow?"

Holly stood absolutely still, rolled her eyes and said, "Get real," and turned away in a hurry. "Oh, never mind, it's only family. They won't notice. May I borrow your curling iron? Mine's on the fritz. I'd like to take along your black beach robe, the one with the cut-outs, and your white sandals."

Libby's response was lost in the scraped vegetables. She didn't hear Hazelwood behind her until his voice cut into the silence.

"Lib, I let myself in. No one answered the bell. You getting deaf?"

She whirled around to see her former husband, the girls' father, in the center of the kitchen, looking like he had never left. His damp hair curled itself, fresh from the shower. She looked at his sweet mouth speaking to her in rolling southeast Missouri sounds. His southern drawl she missed the most.

Tears formed in her eyes on this cold December day where the stillness of the frozen ground outside reminded her of a season that belonged to her in both old and new ways. Hazelwood's shirt collar stood white and starched above the crew neck of his green sweater. His leather coat smelled strong and male, and she knew without a doubt his body would feel as soft and hard and wonderful as it had in the beginning. Why did she do this to herself? Her new life was good. She liked her job.

"Oh, Haz, I'm getting ready for the family tomorrow. You know how frantic I get." She rubbed the backs of her wet hands against her flour-powdered apron. He startled her with his unannounced presence. She hated, yet loved, the way he slouched against the door frame in her kitchen.

"Doing it all as usual, huh? You look like you need some rest. Why don't you take a vacation, get away. Kitchen smells good." He moved closer to her, leaned forward and said, "So do you. Are my girls ready? Carrots need salt," he added, as he reached across her for the saltshaker, tasted a carrot from the dish, and managed to drop a second one on the hot stove burner to sizzle. The singed-carrot smell conflicted with the aroma of apples cooking on another burner.

Before Libby responded, their youngest daughter, Anne, rushed into the room. She slipped her arms around her mother's waist, hugged her. "Bye, Mom. You have a wonderful Christmas. We'll call if we can get through."

Libby dried her hands and untied her apron for a proper good-bye, but the two of them were already arm and arm on their way to the car.

"Wait, Anne, your pink sweater." Her words fell flat in a now empty room. She heard the front door close with enough force to rattle painted plates on the plate rail. She didn't remember Holly's good-bye at all. They were gone just like that. South for the holiday. She shivered and returned to the kitchen to scrub the tiled floor and wonder why she ached to cry.

On Christmas morning, Libby was up by six. She hauled the chilled turkey from the refrigerator and plopped it into her mother's dark enamel pan. She washed bags of cranberries and left them in the strainer. The backyard was visible from the kitchen window over the sink where she worked. Flower barrels stood empty. They waited like hopeful old maids. She knew in spring tulip bulbs would emerge from those same barrels, that awhile ago they housed a circle of promise, pink impatiens. The rose bushes stuck out their hard, skinny branches, brown and thorny, while juniper trees bowed green, home to a bold red cardinal and his counterpart, the pale female. The ground beneath the juniper hid under a protected mat of dropped needles, nature's featherbed.

She shook yeast granules into a clean, empty, mayonnaise jar, added tepid water, and watched instant bubbles appear and dissolve themselves into a muddy liquid ready to roll down the sifted flour that waited in peaks in her largest mixing bowl. She stirred and shaped the rolls, placed them on top of the dryer to rise, and covered them with a thin hotel towel, one Hazelwood had brought home from his travels. A stolen towel covered the tender rolls. That somehow said a lot about their relationship. He brought home things she did not like, covered her vulnerable parts with objects to make up for parts of himself he could not share.

Cranberries bubbled in sugar water and burst into a red ruby aroma that hovered over the kitchen like an old friend. She forgot to make the cranberries with a sugar substitute. From what she could remember, Uncle Harold never took cranberries anyway. Hard, it was hard to please everyone. Is that what she tried to do? No, she only wanted things to be nice in the same way her grandmother did. Grandmother Brooks made biscuits with crusty bottoms and soft tops. Her sister had always eaten the browned bottoms, and Libby preferred the soft counterparts. Her grandmother had pleased the both of them.

Dinner was almost done. She set the table with her mother's dishes bought with hay money in Memphis, Tennessee. They were ivory colored with pink blossoms, birthday dishes, special-occasion dishes for family parties. Her mother gave her the dishes when she started having the family dinners.

Running her hand across the glazed roses, her mother had said, "Libby, I know you will take care of them, love them the way I have, and don't ever put them in the dishwasher!"

The phone interrupted her thoughts. Libby heard her daughter's voice. "Mom, this is Holly. It's great here. We're on our way to the beach."

"Holly, don't forget sunguard—dark-skinned persons need protection, too."

"Dad's chartering a fishing boat. You know he's not drinking. Sober as a judge. Oh, Mom, we miss you."

"Me, too, honey. Have fun."

"Hey wait, before we hang up. Dad wants to say something."

"Lib, this is a great place. Fly down, join us."

She heard his words, admired them, and remembered how quickly some flowers died when cut, like iris that always are better left in the yard. "Hazelwood, do you think I can drop everything, fly down like that? What about my plans here? My reality is here. Sorry."

He was quiet for a moment, the miles between them stretched like worn elastic that had no bounce back to it. He knew. She was sure of that.

"Okay, you're right, Lib. Have a great holiday."

The silence became hers again. Inside she twitched with sadness. She wondered who the dry sober Hazelwood was. She could visualize the three of them soaking up sunshine; Holly, dark and mysterious looking, and Anne, the daughter with small hands and size-four dresses, tagging behind, her fair hair fanning across her face in the breeze. Hazelwood would wear cut-offs and a bandana tied through his hair, and would be, like the girls' friends, already varnished tan. She could smell his damp skin, after a shower before bed, when he slept beside her, barely moving throughout the night. It was she who wrestled the covers and tossed in her dreams. She didn't want to sleep with Haz anymore.

A woodpecker clutched the trunk of a tree outside the kitchen window. He rapped repeatedly against the barren ash. His scarlet head nodded as he picked at and won insects crouched in the bark crevices for safety. There would be tropical birds in the Cayman Islands, but exotic blues and greens couldn't be as beautiful as this creature in her own yard. Great tree limbs held in a wind which lowered the temperature. She went into the living room to turn on the jet under the hickory logs.

The fire crackled and by two o'clock a red candle dripped warm wax. Shadows flickered in the hall across from the tree with miniature lights. She added another log to the fire and then she showered and dressed in her long black skirt and a blouse with a large white collar. Her pearls cooled her neck. The doorbell sounded as she finished dressing.

Her mother entered first. She carried one pie. Her father carried the other pie swaddled in a checkered cloth, laid in a sweetgrass basket. He bore his cargo like a man bringing home his firstborn.

"Libby, this here is pumpkin pie, but the one your dad has, the pecan one, is like you wanted when you were little. Your Uncle Harold picked every last pecan. Watch for shells."

Libby studied her mother's flushed face. Her cheeks were dabbed with rouge and her lipstick inclined to leave the line of her lips, leak into the tender flesh around her mouth. Yet she sparkled in the candlelight, an ornament herself.

Aunt Peg carried in a load of presents, and her cousin Rob arranged them under the tree. He didn't hurry. Her bachelor Uncle Harold stood by the fire and rubbed his red-knuckled fingers. His usual Christmas envelopes bulged under his coat.

Libby noticed that the stranger, their guest Isaac, still fussed in the closet, beset with the task of hanging up coats and scarves. She moved closer to the closet doorway and was surprised to find the man from her uncle's apartment building scarcely older than she, late forties, perhaps. He tilted his head, ran his hand through dark thick hair, and at the same time extended his other open hand. His touch felt warm. His hand covered hers briefly with a firm gentleness.

"Hope I'm not too much trouble, an extra dinner guest."

"No, you're fine. My mom prepared a special fish casserole for you."

Isaac colored slightly. His red scarf still encircled his neck. For some reason, Libby laughed like a giddy young girl.

"Too much holiday," she echoed on her way to the kitchen for the punch. She served the crystal cups and sank into the flowered couch in front of the now hearty fire. Her father sat next to her. He draped his lanky arm across the back of the couch and stroked the back of her hair for a minute. She looked at her father and smiled.

"Nice here in your home," her father offered. "Cozy."

Isaac, the stranger, leaned back in a chair in the corner. He held his punch with both hands, ducked his head now and then for a sip of the fruity drink. Libby liked the chair he claimed. Funny how no one, other than herself, ever chose to sit there. Windows flanked the chair. You could see the south side of her yard and the west side. West . . . the direction she planned to take her life and still would like to visit, places far away from southeast Missouri.

They all looked at her now, waited for her to orchestrate the next move. The room glowed. The couch cushioned her lower back. She watched the fire spit in the grate. The best part was that the work was done. Now there would be a leisurely dinner and presents afterwards. She would fix tidy packets of leftovers for everyone to take home, except the fish casserole. She would keep that and ask Isaac to stay for supper. She noticed that he had taken a book from her bookshelf and was reading. It was a book entitled *North American Birds and Their Habitats*. In the distance she heard the rat-a-tat-tat of the backyard woodpecker, faithful to this season year after year.

"Isaac," she called from across the room. Her parents, aunt, cousin, and uncle turned in unison to look at him. They seemed to be holding their breath. No, it was she who was doing that. "Isaac, where are you from?"

"Oregon," he answered.

"What are you doing in the Midwest?"

"I'm on sabbatical from the university to study the Little Blue Heron of Missouri."

Libby leaned back, let her eyelids lower. She could almost hear long-legged birds flap their wings and rise into the sky. She smelled the marshy bottomlands, the bayou places they selected. She looked at Isaac more closely. Here sat a man who spent time watching birds, and was studying the birds of her childhood.

"Is it lonely?" she asked.

"Do you mean do I get lonely? Sometimes. Patience and time. It takes that. You can't hurry birds. When you enter their landscape, you have to remember it's their landscape."

Libby nodded and got up from her place by the fire, moved toward the kitchen. Isaac followed. His footsteps echoed throughout the house, firm footsteps, steady like the hardwood floors he crossed.

He asked, "How may I help?"

She handed him dishes of sweet potatoes, apples, and a platter of cornbread and sorghum molasses on the side. The others came to the kitchen, one by one, to carry their share to the dining room table, covered with her mother's damask tablecloth. They stood together and joined hands for prayers of thanks. There was comfort in the rhythm of the family, similar to the repeated sounds of the woodpecker who returned to be heard, a part of every Christmas gathering.

May Day King

"Sunny, you'll forget him. Give yourself some time."

"This is different, Mama. Don't you see? John Paul is dead. I didn't know he was going to die."

"You'll find another nice boy to care about. You are thirteen years old. How much does thirteen know about being in love?"

"A lot. I intend to care about John Paul Sloan for the rest of my life. He deserves a lifetime of someone's love."

Sunny's mother looked at her daughter. She bit her lower lip and sighed as she cradled her right arm in her left. "Pains you still, his dying that way?"

Sunny nodded. Her lips clamped shut.

"Sure, honey, it hurts. Tell me how it hurts."

Sunny placed her hand over her mid-chest and drew in her breath. "I see him everywhere. He's out in the yard, up by the school, in the road, and in my dreams. He stands there in his May Day suit, the one the teacher bought him. Mama, she went down to J.C. Penney's . . . she never knew she was buying a funeral suit. I think John Paul was handsome on May Day, don't you?"

"Sure he was. Nice for his people he had a suit to get laid out in. And listen to me, Sunny, you picked him to be your King. He was King for a day on account of you."

"I picked John Paul to be my escort, my King, because he was most likely to never be a real life King. They are so poor,

Mama. Sloans are about the poorest people in the school."

"How do you know the meaning of poor? People like the Sloans with ten kids have each other."

"You know they live in that old ramshackle house that straddles the ditch dump. Welfare buys their school lunches. John Paul was never going to be no real life King."

"You were beautiful in your pink ruffled gown. I thought you were the loveliest girl I'd ever seen. I stood in back by the schoolroom door before the procession started. When I saw the sunshine skip over your blond hair, and you in that petal-pink dress, tears ran down my face. Mothers feel that way when their kids show themselves all grown up, and maybe it helped to have those magnolias blooming in the school yard."

"When I'm at school, I always look at those magnolias. I half expect to see him there . . . John Paul . . . by the stone bench. That was where the procession started. He never held my hand, since it was a school thing, but his coat sleeve brushed my hand when we walked to the throne. He didn't know I loved him. I did. We didn't talk. We looked at each other in arithmetic. Did you know he was the smartest and the very best looking boy in our class? I thought he looked regal in the May Day ceremony. But at the funeral he seemed to be gone. Know what I mean? He didn't look like himself at all. Do people who drown always look that way?"

"I don't know, honey. I think he looked gone because his soul heard the calling and left his body way before we passed his coffin. Maybe it left even before his body washed ashore."

"Fishing . . . How come his daddy took him fishing in a boat when he couldn't swim?"

"I don't know. His daddy must carry the most pain of all, swelled up inside of him with no place to go."

Sunny held her head in her hands. Her mother reached out and stroked her hair. "He lived longer than some," she said. "He connected with you, with your feelings. Some never do that."

"Was in his eyes, I saw life. We met in his eyes. We didn't have many words to say."

"That's being young, Sunny. Words come when the growing is done. But, see here, the boy is dead. It's time to get on with you. You have to say your goodbyes to John Paul. See, it's like you got this invisible cord attached to him. You keep pulling him back. That's the part in your head imagines you see him. Let's go up to your school, and you call him out of your head. Give him your goodbyes."

"That's scary, Mama. I feel silly."

They walked together to the school. No one was there. Magnolia blossoms littered the ground. They sat on the stone bench where the branches hung down so low that Sunny could barely see the length of the schoolyard. She waited. A noon train whistled past on its way to New Orleans. Sunny leaned against the trunk of the tree. She closed her eyes. A long way off she thought she heard notes from "Pomp and Circumstance." She opened her eyes and strained to see the schoolyard. In her mind's eye, she saw a smiling John Paul remove his brown suit coat. He laid it on the clover patch beside the old swing set. He unbuttoned his starched white shirt and rolled up his sleeves.

Sunny cried. She thought she saw John Paul run across the sweet yard of school days. He turned and waved before he seemed to disappear.

Sunny jumped up. She ran across the open yard. She heard herself say, "Goodbye. I loved you John Paul Sloan." She ran until her eyesight was clear and her breath was only big enough to whisper to herself. "Yes, I know, you loved me, too."

Sunny's mother picked two bachelor buttons on her way across the schoolyard. She handed Sunny the prettiest flower. Sunny stuck it in her hair. Their arms interlocked as they walked toward home.

CHRISTMAS SEQUINS

My new stepmother wore a knit suit from Goldsmith's. It was a shade of Christmas green that matched her emerald ring. My dress was black and strapless with sequins across the bodice. It was pencil-thin with a kick pleat in back. I felt cold and uncomfortable riding in the backseat of Daddy's car. My father drove fast on country roads and smoked cigars with the windows closed. We were on the way to the farm for Christmas dinner at my grandmother's.

My sister, Dixie Lou, wore her flared wool skirt and a pink cashmere sweater with choker pearls from Woolworth's. Daddy's wife gave her the cashmere and our mama picked out the pearls. I bought my dress, on sale at Ward's, with Christmas shopping money.

Mama said before we left the house with our father and his new wife, "That dress is not appropriate for you to wear to your grandmother's for Christmas. It's an after-five dress, a cocktail party dress. Sixteen-year-olds have no business in a dress like that."

"You said we were old enough to choose our outfits. I want to wear this dress. Daddy's wife will be dolled up."

My mother didn't say another word. She just helped herself to another piece of Christmas kuchen and stirred her coffee into circles.

When we pulled into the driveway at my grandparent's farm house, snowflakes scurried about the back stoop. I heard wind whip the heavy sheets of plastic my grandfather used to cover the screen porch in winter. The porch's linoleum floor-covering looked worn, but my grandmother kept it spotless in spite of Missouri mud tracked in from the fields.

The kitchen, heated by a wood cook stove, held the aroma of baked chicken, cornbread dressing, biscuits with soft tops and crusty bottoms, cured ham, and sweet potatoes. We passed through rooms with no heat, until we reached the front room with plank flooring, a horsehair sofa, two rocking chairs, an oak table, lamp, and an oil stove that grumbled in the corner.

My grandfather sat in one of the rocking chairs in Sears' cotton pants, suspenders, and a matching gray shirt. The clock ticked, and the stove sent out a circle of warmth. The couch against the wall scratched me when I sat down, and I felt the shoulder of cold descend from the tall ceiling. My uncles wore sweaters and sport coats. Daddy had on a three-piece, charcoal-gray suit with a red Windsor-knotted tie. My skin, above my strapless dress, grew goose bumps, and my legs shivered beneath my sheer hose. The grown-ups talked.

"Well, George B., how's business? Are you selling many of those John Deere tractors?" my grandfather asked my father.

"Business is good, Poppa. Are you about ready to get one?"

"Got a good team of mules, don't need any five-thousand-dollar tractor."

Quiet hung around the room without a Christmas tree, where a faded picture of Jesus, as a child, hung above the piano, and a huge bowl of oranges and nuts graced a table decorated with a crocheted doily.

Uncle Winfield interrupted the silence. "Ruth, want to take a walk with me to the barn?"

I looked down at my stiletto heels and thought of the snow. He looked at my feet, too, and said, "I got some old army boots 'bout fit you."

It wasn't long before he came back into the room and got down on his knees to help me get the boots laced up around my ankles. I put on my dress-up mouton coat, and we headed outside. When I passed my stepmother's chair by the stove, she made the strangest face. Her Tabu perfume followed us to the door.

We stopped under the pecan tree in the backyard, and Uncle Winfield scratched away snow to pick up one forgotten nut. He handed me the cold pecan, and I put it in my pocket.

"Your mama used to pick up buckets of pecans out here when you were a kid."

The silky rayon skirt of my dress felt like a sheet of ice wrapped around my lower body. My teeth chattered on the way to the barn. *Remember when you were a kid* paraded across my mind.

"You look grown-up today. Real pretty dress. Too bad you didn't wear warmer clothes so I could take you for a ride to the river to get more cottonwood, but I don't think you'd want to get your dress messed up."

I looked down at the shiny black of my skirt blotched with huge snow flakes. I wondered if my dress would look all right when it dried. *Dressing up . . . dressing up . . .* part of growing up.

"Do you have a pair of overalls in the barn? I could put them on over my dress."

The barn felt warmer. My uncle handed me overalls and a heavy woolen shirt, and then he went outside to hitch up the mules. I bunched up my dress and pulled on the overalls and the shirt. A few sequins from my dress showed through where a shirt button was missing. One small sequin skittered to the barn floor. I left it there, a perfect circle of glitter.

"Here, let me hoist you up," my uncle offered.

We were in the wagon now. My old uncle didn't shop in the

city or have any business at all. He, the eldest son, stayed duty-bound on the farm, helped his father farm 240 acres of river-bottom land.

The levee's great hill hid, covered by snow, but the team of four mules moved forward in rhythm, worked the snow road, warriors in the wind. At the top of the levee, we paused before we rode down to the low land by the river. Ice rode by in great jiggling mounds, ice castles racing in water. That was the way that I felt, like an ice castle being forced to rush and run to what lies ahead, over-dressed for dinner, not dressed right for winter, not ready yet.

"Beautiful, isn't it?" my uncle said. "All froze up before long, but today she moves along pretty good."

My uncle hauled ready-cut wood onto the wagon while I watched the snow fall. I didn't feel cold anymore, covered with wagon wraps and my uncle's clothes.

Back at the barn, while I waited for my uncle to wipe down the mules, I heard a scratching sound in the tackle room. I peeked through space between the rough log walls to see a striped cat spreading hay all around, while three smaller versions of the mother cat, a trio of kittens, rolled and played in each other's arms. And then, a fourth kitten appeared. She was black with a collar of white sprinkled with dots of black and with a tail tipped in white. She seemed different from the others.

"You take that odd-colored kitten home."

She was a skinny cat, all legs and purrs. She did not seem afraid. I didn't bother to take off my uncle's overalls when we went back to the house. I tucked the kitten under the front of my coat where she batted the flickering light in sequins at the top of my dress.

"See, Daddy, she really wants to come home with me, and Mama won't care."

My father looked at me. It was as though he saw me for the

first time all day. He put his arms around me and hugged me.

"George B., I don't think you ought to let her have that cat," my stepmother said from somewhere across the room. "Maybe we could get her a songbird."

"You really want a cat?" he asked. "Well, why not? Girl needs a pet, and this one needs a home."

Everyone in the room murmured in unison, "Yes, a girl needs a pet."

They all looked at me. I saw my grandfather with the corners of his mouth beginning to turn up. A nod away, my grandmother announced dinner as she brushed flour from her apron. Best of all, my father beamed approval.

We moved into the warm kitchen where everyone sat down together. My grandfather said, "We give thanks, Almighty Lord, for a good year."

My stepmother smiled when Aunt Virginia asked for her ambrosia recipe. It was then that I noticed her eyes looked as pretty a shade of green as the suit she wore.

When I got home that night, I took off my cocktail dress and put it in the back of the closet behind all of my other dresses. It felt too tight, and I didn't think that I could ever dance in it with such a narrow skirt. I put on flannel pajamas and went into the living room to sit with the cat on the floor by the fireplace.

"I think I'll call her Sequin. What do you think, Mama?"

My mother had on her cozy robe with the quilted collar. She looked up from the book she was reading, smiled, and said, "That's fine. Was it cold on the farm? Used to be, unless you stayed out in the kitchen."

"It wasn't bad. Uncle Winfield sent you something." I retrieved the single pecan from my coat pocket and handed it to my mother. "He loaned me some overalls and a wool shirt. Did you know he still has his old army boots? They are great in the snow. I wonder if the thrift shop has any. You should have seen the river with the ice floating by."

My mother sighed as she turned the pecan again and again with her fingers. "Yes, I have seen it. Something different about a farm at Christmas, isn't there? I think that kitten is going to grow up a real city cat, but I doubt she'll forget her beginnings. Yes, why not call her Sequin? She does seem to sparkle. Kittens are so dear. I hope she doesn't grow up too fast."

PLASTIC CURTAINS

The clear plastic curtains in our upstairs apartment living room came from the five-and-dime and were decorated with huge pink painted roses. These window coverings reached from ceiling to floor. Sunshine filtered through pink plastic flowers felt gaudy hot in all seasons. Late afternoons glowed, became a hushed melon color, but nights took on a ghost-like pallor when the moon rose over the Mississippi.

I missed our other house with sleek hardwood floors and crystal chandeliers. That was the "before Daddy left house." My mother rented the apartment after my sister went away to college and my father took a new wife.

Mama said, "We'll rent out the big house and live in a place we can better afford."

The upstairs apartment was in a rambling 1920 brick with a backyard that overlooked the Mississippi River. Mama's friend Leticia, who worked for a shoe store on Main Street, and her two kids lived downstairs. Our place had a private entrance, a long flight of stairs, an entry hall, living room, pantry, kitchen, two bedrooms, pink bath, and an upstairs back porch.

At our other house, my parents played Strauss waltzes. Here, I preferred Joni James, Eartha Kitt, and Nat King Cole. When I liked a particular song, I played it over and over until I wore it out. I liked "Oh Happy Day" after we moved into the apartment. Harold, the current man in my mother's life, hated that song.

"That isn't music," he roared. "Why do you let her play that trash, Hildegarde?"

My mother never answered him. She walked over to the record player and lifted my record off and put on Glenn Miller. Harold played trumpet in a band across the river in southern Illinois at The Purple Crackle. He had a sandy-colored mustache and drove a black Ford. He wasn't divorced like my mother. Harold's wife of many years had died after a lingering illness and left him his trumpet, one son, and a dog. The dog wore a curled lip and a continual growl. The kid was a drip. I didn't speak to him in the halls at school. The very idea that we might become a family made me hot all over, perspire and chill at the same time. My legs became pogo sticks. There was no escape from moments like these, that came frequently when I thought about family.

My bedroom was right off the entry hall. There were twin beds and a modern, gray dresser. The headboards for the beds leaned against magnolia-flower wallpaper. My mother and I didn't have much luck hooking the bedboards onto the metal bed frames. The wool rug was tied, still rolled up, in front of a tower of moving boxes stacked in the corner. My stuff seemed safest left in the boxes since there was no closet in this room.

At night, passing cars tossed bold reflections into my bedroom windows. I pulled blankets up over my head to meet the black night. There was no heat vent in this room. Our grandmother's quilts covered both beds. I missed them both, my grandmother and my sister. Sophia Newcomb was the college my father and his new wife picked out to send my sister to study languages and political science. She was dating a boy whose father owned a coffee plantation. I marked a calendar over my bed, waited for the days until Christmas vacation when my sister would come home with a trunk filled with New Orleans clothes: strapless formal gowns, cashmere sweaters, and tweed skirts. She let me wear anything I wanted, as long as I hung it up afterwards, and was careful not to wrinkle the gowns.

One Friday night, I went to the high-school pep rally and football game. Friends dropped me off afterwards. It was close to eleven when I got home. At the top of the stairs, I hesitated before I opened the door to the living room. I heard soft music. My palm against the doorknob grew damp. I leaned forward, strained to listen, and opened the door. The only light in the room came from a lamp on an end table. Two drinking glasses pooled perfect circles of water next to an ashtray with cigarette butts. Harold smoked Kents. My mother didn't smoke. I took off my jacket and laid it across my sister's glossy piano bench. It swished in a slide to the floor. I coughed and walked into the kitchen, where my mother stood at the sink rinsing something. Her black curly hair looked tousled. Her Merle Norman lipstick was gone. She was barefoot. The back porch door stood ajar. Winter air halted my steps. I guessed that Harold had to be on the back porch. *All right, I can wait you out, Harold.*

I sat down on one of our chrome kitchen chairs. A package of Kents lay open on the table. Minutes froze on the clock above the sink. In time, a red-faced Harold came in from the porch. He ran his hands through his hair and wiped his mouth with a handkerchief. I stared until his squinted eyes met mine. I reached across the table and took his package of cigarettes. I popped one out of the pack the way I had practiced and tapped it several times on the back of my hand. I placed it between my lips, caressed the tip with my tongue, and raised his lighter. Harold watched me draw the smoke in and exhale it into his direction. A muscle in his cheek twitched. My mother's back was still turned. There were no words between the three of us, only the smoke. It curled in the air, rose to the ceiling, and disappeared.

Harold spoke of leaving. My mother followed him into the

living room. I listened to muffled words, their silence, and imagined kissing. My eyes burned before tears gathered in the corners. I snubbed out the hot cigarette and went to bed before my mother returned from saying good-night to Harold.

Several weeks later, my mother traveled to St. Louis on business for her job at the army recruiting office. She planned to be away for a week and decided that at sixteen I was old enough to stay home without her. She did our hand-wash of lingerie on Sunday and hung it on the line in the backyard before she left.

"Don't forget to bring our clothes in tonight," she reminded me.

Night dragged after my mother's bus left the station. I returned to our apartment and turned on all the lights and played a stack of records after supper. I did geometry and European history homework and went to bed after rolling my hair in rag rollers. I listened to cars passing the house. River barges announced their presence with foghorns as they moved south in the night. I slept with a large, stuffed panda bear guarding my back. In the morning before school I fixed myself a decent breakfast of buttered toast and scrambled eggs. I doctored the coffee with half a cup of milk.

Monday evening, my boyfriend, Paul Wayne, came over. We did biology homework and afterwards kissed while we sat on the couch. We drank a soda and fixed popcorn. We were lying on the couch real close when I suddenly remembered that this was the same couch that my father used to take afternoon naps on. He'd put his *St. Louis Post Dispatch* over his chest for warmth and sleep with his glasses on. I didn't want to think about my father.

Paul Wayne had dark hair and hazel eyes. He smelled like Wrigley's gum and soap. He was breathing heavier now, kissing my neck. I thought about Harold. What did my mother see in him? Paul's body was warm against me.

"Wait a minute," I said, as I slithered out from under him and left the living room. My mother's bedroom was dark and cool. I turned on her bedside lamp and opened her maple bureau drawer and lifted out her rose-colored satin lounging pajamas. We were both size eight. My father gave her the pajamas last Christmas. *Oh darling, they are beautiful,* echoed in my mind. The satin slid cool against my skin. I tied the sash around my waist and looked at my flushed face in the mirror. My blond hair shone from the drops of Suave I used every day. I was fair like all of my father's family. I flipped the sides of my hair back, turned off the lamp, and went back into the living room. There was no lamplight now. The moon looked into the window through painted roses on the plastic curtains. Shadows played. Paul Wayne turned on his side to make room for me on the couch. I snuggled against him and didn't move away when he ran his hand across the satin smocking on the front of my mother's best lounging pajamas.

My mother didn't notice her wrinkled pajamas. I hid them in the bottom of her drawer under her granny gowns. She was furious that I had forgotten to bring in the hand-wash all week while she was gone. When she returned from her trip, our panties, bras, and slips were harsh, stiff, and faded from the winter weather. They hung firmly pinned on the revolving clothesline, their delicate softness lost forever. They never were the same, but we wore them anyway.

Harold moved to Texas, and Paul Wayne joined the army and went to Korea after someone in my mother's office recruited him. I grew accustomed to the plastic curtains in the living room after the sun faded the flowers and offered me a better view of the river from the window. There were always seasonal changes on the river, but the thing I missed most when I went off to college was the sound of the riverboat foghorns passing in the night.

GRACE

Brave—she had to be brave, didn't she? If sixteen was old enough to go to work, then she was old enough to ride the bus across the city, even at midnight. Grace looked out of the bus window and watched the street signs. Manchester Street in St. Louis was very busy. Cars flashed by and signal lights changed to light up brick houses and garish shop fronts. She pulled the signal cord and walked to the exit door. She heard the bus doors swish closed behind her. Music floated from Allie's Bar. She dashed across the lit street and looked ahead toward her own front door. Her key etched an imprint in her moist hand. Once inside, Grace took a deep breath. The world out there was sometimes a scary place, but she was at home and safe. She walked up one flight of stairs and turned her key in an apartment door, a two-room efficiency where she, her sister, and her mother were staying for the summer. They all had jobs. In the fall, they would return home to southeast Missouri, to their town which bore no city lights, only lightning bugs with their small flickering lanterns.

Grace emptied her purse on the double bed where her mother and sister slept. Coins jumped out and fell into heaps. She sifted through the money and counted out six dollars, earned in tips at the counter drugstore where she worked. She scooped up the coins and hid them in a sock in the closet.

Her mother and sister weren't home yet. She had the room

to herself. They didn't have a radio, phone, or warm cups of cocoa here. Two pictures decorated the walls. They were copies of *Pinky and the Blue Boy*. Grace turned out the light and raised the window shades to look at lights coming on in the neighboring apartments. "Hello, world, you are beautiful from in here. But when I'm out there I'm scared to death. Standing on the corner, waiting for the bus is the worst of all. Mama says I should look straight ahead. I want to look at people, not at buildings and doors. My boss doesn't seem just right. Rosie and I go down to the locker room together on account of the way he looks at us. We look out for him.

"'Need a ride, Grace?' he asks. 'Give you a lift home, honey?'"

That old man is a real problem. Who are you going to tell when he's your main boss? Mama says he's not about to touch girls on the job. But then, she doesn't work there. She doesn't know how he tries to rub up against you behind the counter.

Daddy always said, "Hold on Grace, it's all you got to go with when a man wants you for life." But Daddy didn't exactly say how to handle men like these. He was talking about young men you felt heart stirrings for. Damn, Daddy, dead you aren't much help to me.

"Open the door, Grace. It's us."

She opened the door for her sister and mother.

"The show was great!" her mother said. "Wish you could have gone."

Grace listened to every word about the movies while they all got ready for bed.

"Mama, you think we could go home about August? I got six dollars today."

"Good. Save it for school clothes. You know we got to stay until the end of summer. How was work?"

"Good, but I hate the bus ride."

"So what's with the bus ride? Get a way home with someone

you work with."

"Who, Mama?"

"Pick someone who is sober and old enough to do right by you."

"I'm scared."

"Of what?"

"People in the night."

"I can't haul you through life."

"Let me go home."

"Home is here this summer. I know you miss your friends, our house, but try to take a liking to the city."

"Will you come meet me at work tomorrow?"

"Heavens, no, Grace. Go to sleep now."

The next day, Grace studied the drugstore's employees. She decided on asking Mr. Simmons.

"Mr. Simmons, can you give me a ride home tonight, on your way?"

"Sure, Grace, I'd like the company."

Grace leaned back on soft seats in Mr. Simmons's car as he drove through traffic. Simmons was the assistant store manager. His hair was graying at the temples. When he got to Manchester Street, he turned left.

"You turned the wrong way, Mr. Simmons."

He accelerated the car into another lane. "We're stopping off at Rosita's for a pizza. You like pizza, don't you?"

Grace nodded in the dark.

The restaurant's miniature table lights flickered like stars in the night. The pizza was cheese and mushroom, her favorite, but Grace took only one small bite and sipped a Pepsi. Mr. Simmons downed a dark beer and smoked a small cigar in the shadows. He looked at her with black eyes that bore no light. Where had she seen that look before? On the bus? She grew still and looked away. A small muscle twitched at the corner of his mouth.

"Grace, how old are you?"

"Seventeen," she lied. And under her breath she said, "And as mean as a wildcat."

"Like to dance?"

"Sometimes."

"Like to go to parties?"

Before Grace could answer the last question, Mr. Simmons said, "Ever been to Forrest Park?"

"Yes, I mean, no. Is it the zoo?"

"I'm going to show you Forrest Park at night."

"The zoo is closed at night, thank you."

"I know."

Grace put on her mother's face. She stood up and steadied herself against the table that separated her from the man. Her words came hard and fast like taffy boiled too long. "I'm going to leave this place . . . alone . . . and if you follow me, I will scream. I am no baby, but I am no woman yet either. You are going to forget about Forrest Park. If you ever think that again, my Daddy will chase your sorry ass across this city and wipe that look out of your eyes for good. I am as young as your own daughter, as old as my own mother who has told me about ways to stay sixteen, not no sixteen going on thirty-five. Excuse me, Mr. Simmons, but my father waits at my door with a large club."

Grace reached across the table and took the man's cigar out of the ashtray and crushed its hot coal into what remained of his pizza.

She caught the next bus back to Manchester. When she got home, her mother was waiting for her inside the apartment building by the front door. "Gracie, I was worried about you. You're later than usual. Are you all right? You know, I've been thinking, maybe we can go home before school starts so you girls can have some time with your friends."

117

"That's okay, Mama, I can handle it. Not much longer now, is it?"

They hugged and climbed the stairs. Soft city lights flickered through the hall curtains and looked something like lightning bugs around their screen door at home.

My Delta Pearls

Possessions move along with you in life, but there comes a day when you decide to disengage yourself from some of your worldly goods. The keeping and staying of items is decided upon with wisdom. You give some very good things to the children, and also some junk. You keep usable items and comfort yourself with a few choice family pieces, things you will later bequeath to your children. Next, you select a few treasures that for better or for worse will follow you throughout the remaining days of your earthly residency. Special care is given to any item that connects you with the memory of your first love. My Delta pearls fell into this category, a string of pearls with a rhinestone clasp. I always thought that the clasp was a circle of diamonds until one day I looked at it with the aid of a magnifying glass and realized the clasp was made of fragments of glass. The pearls were real. I know this to be a fact because Buddy Powell bought them at a discount store in St. Louis, Missouri, in the 1960s.

On Christmas Eve, he picked me up for our date. He was driving his baby-blue convertible.

"Got something special for you for Christmas. Look in the glove box."

I opened the glove compartment and found two boxes. The first one held a bottle of perfume called My Sin. The second gift was in a blue velvet box shaped like an oyster. The word DELTA was printed in dark blue letters inside the box lid. Nestled against satin lining was a beautiful strand of pearls. Buddy put them on me. They rested cool against my neck.

"I love them," was all I managed. It was snowing and we parked on a dark road. Buddy liked to sit with his arms stretched out on both sides of the front seat. He'd sit there and I'd lean against him and wish he'd kiss me, but Buddy was slow and never seemed to get in a hurry about anything. That evening with the snow outside it looked like dawn instead of ten at night. I knew he was going to ask me to go steady, get pinned or engaged at any minute, so I waited.

"I'm not coming back to school next semester. I'm going to work for my dad till spring and then I'm going to race cars."

"Race cars? Where?"

"All over, south Mississippi. Anywhere they'll have me."

The snow fell all night. The world looked like a great whiteout on Christmas morning. Buddy went home to Portageville and we saw each other a few more times, but he never really came back to me for keeps. Certainly, no man gives a woman perfume and pearls, real pearls at Christmas, unless he loves her, but he never said so in words..

The perfume named My Sin didn't last long and my mother pitched out the empty bottle, but today, the real pearls reside in my top dresser drawer. I wear them during the Christmas season. They're cool on my neck, but strangely hot in the moonlight when it snows, reminiscent of race cars and the kind of men who drive them—slow-talking men who dress their women in jewels, men who like their women smelling sweet and keep their cars moving fast down south where no one wants to be burdened with too many worldly goods, things that could go bad in the heat.

Never A Bastard When Somebody Loves You
Banks of the Mississippi

"Belle, you got to tell Mama and Daddy, you just got to."

"Hush your mouth, Sissy. I can't tell them now. Billy doesn't know."

"Tell Billy. How you going to hide it?"

Belle smoothed the front of her dress. She didn't feel any swelling, but her dress was getting tighter. Her days had passed twice, hadn't they?

"You stop your staring, Sissy. I'm not a monster, you know!"

"How come you didn't do like Mama says and keep yourself pure?"

"I'm not going to try to explain everything to no fifteen-year-old. I always did like Mama said until I got in love with Billy. See, Sissy, not love like for our kin, but star-shining love on a clear summer night."

Sissy looked at Belle, but her sister was gone clean out of herself, staring straight ahead. Sissy followed Belle's gaze with her own toward the river, into the water that lay not three feet away.

Belle's lips quivered. "I don't want to make no man marry me."

"You're the prettiest girl I ever did see, Belle. Mama says you're rich as cow's cream. Billy never stops staring all over you when

121

you're minding your business. I've seen it. Don't you know he's got to marry you? No bastard child, Belle."

"Shut up, Sissy, you don't know. Won't be no bastard child no matter what. Never. This child will be born to me, a woman who loves her. Nobody's a bastard who is loved."

Sissy knelt and picked up a jagged rock and hurled it into the foaming muddy water. "Remember when we were kids and thought we could toss enough stones into this here water to fill it up and make it stop, but there was always new river coming from way up north?" Sissy stepped closer to her sister. "When's the baby coming?"

"March or April, I think."

"Tell Billy tonight." Sissy laid her hand on her sister's arm. "Please."

That evening, Belle brushed the gleam in her hair, the gleam that must have been born to her, "a gift of sun on her hair," her father said. She put on her Sunday blue to wait for Billy to come by after the hay baling. There wasn't one breath of air in the house, so she waited on the front steps.

Billy came across the yard. His arms were brown from summer work, but against the fallen night they looked frightfully white and strong. Belle lost the breath she was holding when Billy sat down beside her.

"Billy, I been waiting since the sun set to see you and tell you . . ."

"Since when did I ever stop work at sundown? Girl, I got exciting news. I'm going to my uncle's in New York next week. He's sick and needs me to work the herd. Guess I'll be up there all winter and maybe next spring."

"Can I go with you?"

"I'll be working rough like. No place for a woman!"

"But I love you."

Billy pulled Belle to his side and captured her rigid body with his arm. "I'll be coming back richer, stronger, and, well, maybe even smarter. Don't know much about dairy herds, but cows up there got these great white barns and people there got more than a string of cotton rows."

"What about me?"

"I love you, girl. I'm coming back. Don't hold me like no kite string. It's for us, for us, something good to grow on."

"I won't hold you down, only close."

He was going away. The lightning bugs flashed on and off on the lawn, somehow like her love for Billy … on … off … on … off. She wanted to punch him and yell, TRAITOR! Instead, she cried the tears Billy kissed and mistook for a woman's way of taking on the newness of separation and waiting.

Billy left.

Several days later, Belle took on the telling of her predicament to her daddy. He didn't yell or rage around at all. His eyes opened full, blue and distant, and attended to looking at Belle only briefly before his shoulders drooped and he walked into the woods. Not one word did he give her before he moved into the cover of the cottonwood trees to hide his disappointment. But then she had never promised him she would stay his little girl. Her womanhood came down between them with razor sharpness. Billy's woman now and soon someone's mother.

Belle's mother said, "We'll make do, and your daddy will get over it. Keep out of his way. Give him a spell. Should have told your boy. He'd a married you and made things right."

Sissy stood with her head down. She saw her mother's callused no-nonsense hands, spinach-cutting hands, hoe-holding hands, twist her good handkerchief into knots. And for the first time, she saw the cold adventure of life creep into her mother's eyes. They had become dark circles admitting not one beam of light.

She turned to see her sister hesitate in the doorway. Belle's slim legs bent slightly like a fawn ready to flee. Her eyes were the most incredible blue, and when she turned to run, her body almost floated down the path toward the river. Sissy followed her sister. The roar of the water silenced their speech and curtained the sound of Belle's sobs. Sissy lay down close to her sister. Sadness flowed eternally from way up north, never ending, even though they had thrown childhood's collection of rocks into the water.

The baby was born in mid-April, very small, and with hair that shone like Belle's. Belle died shortly after the child arrived.

Belle's daddy cried. Belle's mother cried. Sissy covered Belle's body with the family afghan, covered the not-so-old, not-so-young body.

"Belle, what did you go and die for?" Sissy whispered to her sister. "Girl, pretty one. You are leaving me . . . and her. I hate you leaving me here. Always we was two but one together. Now, who will be the mother woman? Me? I guess me. I promise you . . ." Sissy covered her sister's paleness. She turned to her mother's tears, and reached out her arms to take the child. Now her mother could devote her whole being to grieving fully for the one under the afghan. The baby was silent and warm. She nestled against Sissy's budding breasts. Sissy swayed with the child until the oak floorboards beneath her sang a lullaby. Under the eaves of the house, the wind echoed again and again, "She won't be a bastard. Remember, not love for your kin, but love like star shining on a clear summer night."

The baby was named Sarah Sue in honor of her great-grandmother. Her body filled out and took on a ripe rosy roundness. Her cornflower blue eyes flirted with every new sound and sight.

"Blue's definitely her color, wouldn't you say, Sissy? Don't you think I could make her a little dress out of that piece of goods in your drawer? I mean, for the picnic at Cottonwood Point on Sunday."

"Oh, Mama, do you think we really ought to take her? I don't know what to say to all those folks about Sarah."

"She's going to go. No folks going to make me hide in this here bayou forever. Lord knows we got little enough company save ourselves. We are all going."

Sunday came. It was one of those bright bold days. A light breeze fluttered over the sandbar where the picnic crowd settled in. Sissy carried her small charge nestled against her neck. She felt her own heart beating in her chest, ears, and for heaven's sake, even in her eyes. Her mama trailed behind her, stopping to visit with all of her neighbors, like a woman gathering eggs on a rich summer day. Sissy stopped and stood still. Sarah's blue dress billowed in the wind as the river rode by with whipped cream caps.

"There she is. There's that baby! Sure is pretty, favors Belle, I'd say."

"Oh, Sis, let us have a chance to hold the youngun. Come on, baby, I am your old Aunt Lottie."

Sissy handed Sarah to Lottie. Others waited to see . . . touch . . . hold . . . to love the baby. They clucked, cooed, and craned to see. How old they all looked, wrinkled farm folk with speckled hands, Cottonwood Point people. These folks were beholden to their land which somehow failed to speak to their children, the new generation, most of whom fled to the towns with the boxed factories.

Sarah was cooed to, sung to, and held for the remainder of the day. When the sun slipped down, Sissy lay on a pallet with Sarah, to listen to her elders who were talking, talking, talking. She never remembered what they said for sure, but it sounded like . . . no bastard child ever . . . if someone loves you. And the river moved on past Cottonwood Point's campfire light where the women lingered on the edge of night with their little ones drowsing under someone's grandmother's quilt and the men knotted in their own groups of noisy exchange. The sandbar jutted into muddy water warmed by a whole summer of sunshine, and no one was in any hurry to leave until late into the night.

FIFTEEN YEARS LATER

William Robert Warren tightened his grip on the steering wheel of his 1951 Chevrolet. He blocked his feelings, bottled up like the August heat of cotton country. His thoughts drifted back to the year of her birth . . . 1936. "A daughter," he said aloud to himself, as the incredible smothering hot seeped from his pores and formed droplets across his face.

Aside the road, signs announced the southeast Missouri Bootheel towns of Sikeston, Hayti and Portageville. He blinked through his sweat and turned off Highway 61 South to buy gas in Caruthersville.

Sarah was born at Cottonwood Point. He had never seen her, but he remembered the making, the mating. He had loved her mother, still did, would never have left her in this rotten, bloody, cotton bayou if he had known.

He accelerated the car and turned into a Phillips 66 gas station. A man appeared immediately. He waited by the pump until Bill Warren got out of his car.

"Want to fill up?"

Bill nodded as he thrust his hands into the pockets of his baggy trousers.

"Nice car. Brand new, I'd say!"

"That's right."

"See you're from New York."

Bill glanced at his license plate. New York never had dust like this. There were green mountains upstate with forests of needle pines and lakes of frigid water. Folks minded their own business the same as their forefathers minded theirs. But here even a gas station proprietor would have it all, wring every last word out of you. Bill was suddenly aware of the old man's watery eyes. There was no malice, only curiosity born of boredom, straight like the highway that was behind him, and stretched out ahead, flat, long and narrow.

"Visiting folks here?"

"I'm going to the Point to see my daughter."

"Who's that?"

"Sarah Snow."

"Oh, Chastity Snow's girl . . ."

"No, her niece."

"Rightly so, rightly so."

Bill Warren extended his hand. "I'm Bill Warren."

"Wesley Warren's son? I knew old Wesley when you were but a whippersnapper. Both your folks dead now, right?"

Bill nodded as the old man replaced the gas cap. "Say now, we got County Fair next week. You best stay awhile. I'm going to give you some complimentary tickets."

"Thanks. County Fair . . . guess I been to a lot of those when I was a kid." Bill Warren put the tickets into his wallet and started the car engine. To himself he thought about fair freaks. Grandpa Warren had taken him to see the freak show.

"Now Billy Bob, you look around out here until I come back."

Grandpa Warren had disappeared behind a flap at the rear of the tent where a sign read, "No Children Admitted." Billy Bob knew that was the place where the bearded woman and the pinhead men waited. Billy Bob had plenty to see in the main tent.

There was a table with the bottled babies. Those little babies were floating in water with their bellies swollen like dead catfish from the Mississippi.

One of the fair people barked, "See this scientific exhibit of twin babies joined to one body with two heads. Praise the lord folks, that you can donate a little money to this exhibit, the most unusual one of its kind in the country. Move on, boy, so some others can see."

Billy Bob stood mesmerized by the bobbing, floating rhythm of the bottled babies. Sweat ran down his neck as stomach spasms threatened to bring his breakfast up. He twisted his mouth and reeled around and ran from the tent. Grandpa Warren found him at a stand on the crowded midway, throwing hard balls at wooden milk bottles. He won a celluloid kewpie doll on a stick. She had a feather stuck in a band on her head.

Bill Warren stared into the road before him. Six more miles and he would be at Cottonwood Point where he and his father before him were born. His daughter, too, born outside a marriage. He wiped the moisture from his face with the back of his hand. At Gin Junction he would stop for a Nehi soda. Gin Junction consisted of a general store, a school house, and a cotton gin— the money machine of the area. Bill Warren entered the store, letting the screen door bang behind him. He found the soda cooler in the corner where it had always been. He retrieved a dripping Nehi to take to the counter. On the wall behind the cash register he was startled to see war posters. Didn't they know this was 1951?

The storekeeper's eyes followed his gaze to the wall.

"I keep them there to remind folks we ain't never ever safe and free unless we fight for it, fight for this here great American country of ours. That'll be two cents extra if you've a mind to take the bottle with you."

Bill Warren paid the two cents. "Safe and free" drove him from the store and out into the bright "great American country of ours." He kicked the right front tire of his car before he slid in behind the steering wheel. He took one long drink from the soda, got out and placed the sweating bottle on the porch of the general store. He saw the storekeeper's reflection in his rear-view mirror as he drove away. He stood on the porch waving, "Your two cents, mister, here's your two cents from the bottle deposit."

Honesty, purity, and cotton galled up inside of him. He pulled his car off the road when waves of nausea seized him and he stuck his head out of the car window and vomited the orange Nehi onto crusty ground. He wiped his mouth with a white linen handkerchief which bore his initials and then he continued and drove two more miles.

He failed to notice the paint-starved shacks. What he did see in the distance was the Snow home, white against lush green cottonwood tree foliage, but a few hundred yards away. His heart pounded. The car windows were closed now, to block dust which followed him. Sweat rolled down his armpits. The slick, plaid seat covers in his new car grew damp. They smelled ripe. He rolled right past the house and drove to the south-forty, hidden behind the levee, got out of his car and walked to the sandbar which jutted peninsula-fashion into the Mississippi river. Foamy water babbled against the sandy shore. He became a small boy again. He removed his clothes and tossed them into the passing water. Naked and vulnerable, he watched his clothes ride away. They were sucked under when they left him. He straightened his body toward the sun before he opened the car trunk and removed his bag. He dressed in a blue Brooks Brothers suit and knotted a burgundy tie before he combed his hair. From his bag he removed a fat envelope of money which he placed inside his coat. He was ready now, ready to become Sarah's father.

He Never Looked Back

All she loved was walking out the door. The screen banged once for him and once for her. Out he went in his good blue suit. The sun broke through bold cottonwood leaves and played in a sulky wind. Flies glistened, small jewels here and there amongst the marigolds. Gnats crowded around her perspiration. She felt the coolness of her body under her dress and her heart running fast. Her face felt flushed and she knew her socks fell into her shoes.

Today, he was going. She felt like a miniature girl-woman. He was leaving her first lipstick and her new bought pumps. He was leaving her face with the red pimple bumps that appeared in the night when her dreams tried to resolve the longings and loneliness of turning fourteen.

She had her best wave ready. She held her arm in mid-air and waited for him to turn around and look back. Her knees wobbled back and forth, and for heaven's sake, all of a sudden her teeth chattered in spite of the August sun daggers.

He walked faster now toward his old blue Chevrolet, reached his car, and got in without looking back. She heard the car motor begin. She dropped her arm to her side. Her hand found the material of her dress and held on. She lowered her eyelids, and when she opened her eyes again, her father was gone. Her knees got all still. The sun paused behind a cloud and from somewhere a little breeze ran by. She turned and walked back into the house. Her mouth was quiet but her mind was making words and saving thoughts. She lay down on the couch in front of the good black fan, and as the air raced over her, sadness rose and settled in the room on tables and chairs like particles of mad dust. She slept until she heard her mother in the kitchen, shuffling pots and pans in preparation for dinner.

The smell of fried chicken was good. It was her favorite and she felt hungry. At the dinner table, the others, her mother, grandmother, and sister spat their angry words.

"Good riddance," they said.

"Don't waste any tears on him."

"He will burn in hell for sure."

They spoke of her father whose very being now became hard creases in their faces. "Never mind, pet, he isn't worth it. Now dry your tears. You're a big girl now."

All of her sadness and all of her sorrow rose up again like a swollen river. She stood and hurled a chicken leg at the nearest wall. She turned and left the room. The grease stain on the wall remained and reminded her of a hot August day when sweat and tears ran free and her father wore his best blue suit out into the heat of the day.

G.B.

G.B. sat on his wrap-around front porch reading *The Memphis Commercial Appeal*. The walnut tree was within view and the soybeans looked good, but needed a rain. He glanced at his watch and yelled, "Lizzie, come out here right now."

Lizzie opened the back screen door. "What you want, G.B.?"

"Pack our bags. We can just about make the first showing of *Rain Man* in Memphis, if we hurry."

"Oh, G.B., that's a good four-hour drive . . . to see a movie?"

G.B. rubbed his freckle-spotted hands over his ruddy bald head and pursed his lips to a pout.

Lizzie—Elizabeth to her bridge-club friends—removed her smock apron and smoothed her hair at the same time. "Okay, honey, I'm with you. Want to take the girls along?"

"They can go if they can get ready in fifteen minutes. And, Lizzie, fix us a lunch. It's a poor farm boy traveling today."

Lizzie smiled and sighed. G.B. was going to be in one of his frugal moods this trip. The hotel wouldn't be The Peabody. The taxis would go by, and she and G.B. would be walking and taking buses. She looked out to the land, a thousand acres spread before her. There was no need to be frugal anymore, but G.B. had to remind them that he hadn't always been a well-to-do farmer. He started in the depression when farms got bought on promises. G.B., a poor farm boy, amassed a fortune buying and selling, clearing and working land along the banks of the Mississippi

River. He engineered his dreams into their final product. His land was some of the richest delta farmland in the area.

Lizzie smiled to herself when she thought of G.B., nearly fifty years old, still having a love affair with his land. He'd squat down out in the field to look at the crops, feel the rich soil with a practiced hand. His prayers were for rain, or not so much rain, or no rain at all. His moods followed the cycle of the weather.

They packed their bags and the dark Mercedes-Benz pulled out of the drive within the hour. Dixie Lou was G.B.'s eldest daughter, nearly twenty, and Ruth Ann was eighteen. The girls had long ago learned not to question their father's travel plans. They went along because they knew that traveling with G.B. was an adventure.

"Remember that time," Dixie Lou asked, "we went to south Texas to pick oranges and sit in the sun?"

"I well do," Lizzie said. "In those days your papa was a poor farmer with a few dollars in his pocket. He still knew how to have a good time."

G.B. cleared his throat and adjusted his glasses as the black car curled around the curves toward the flatlands of southern Missouri and Arkansas. The group rode in silence until the cotton fields of Sikeston, Missouri, arrived. The flat country went on forever. A rare shack or shanty disrupted the rich and powerful cut of the land.

G.B. pulled the car off the road and down into the guts of a farm field. He stopped in front of a cheerless, paint-free house. The windows were open holes. The porch leaned and swayed like a broken-down mule.

"Look at this shack, girls. The house I was born to wasn't much more. We lived in a dog-trot house. The open hall in between was where the dogs slept."

The girls tried to imagine their father as a boy. His pictures showed him to be small for his age, with horn-rim glasses. He wore overalls. In family photos he always hung onto his mother. G.B. was the baby, spoilt rotten by this large-boned German mother, sheltered and pampered long after his siblings adapted to the hard knocks of the world. G.B. was a dreamer, a book lover and shy to the physical work of the farm. He was scared of one thing, his own father, who disciplined him with cool blue eyes. No words were necessary. G.B. did terrible things as a boy. When he was eleven, he had borrowed his mother's car, a new roadster she purchased with her egg money, and learned to drive on country roads. The driving ended when G.B. took his father out. He stopped suddenly. His father was thrown against a windshield and suffered a broken nose.

"Come on, G.B.," Lizzie now said, "let's get back on the main road. The girls have seen enough deserted shacks for one trip."

G.B. moved onto the highway again. His next stop was a fruit and vegetable stand along the road. "Howdy," G.B. drawled. "How much you selling those tomatoes for?"

"Oh, I can let you have two pounds for a dollar, I guess."

"Give me six-bits worth."

The weathered man surveyed G.B. and his fine car. "Yes, sir, right now."

"How you doing with your stand, captain?" G.B. asked.

"Oh, all right. I guess a little slow this week."

"I always wanted to run a roadside stand," G.B. said.

"Funny you'd say that when I always wanted to drive a car like this one."

"Tell you what, you take my car for one hour, and I'll run your stand for you."

The fruit-stand man looked at G.B. very carefully. "It's a deal."

Lizzie looked ruffled, but got out of the car and told the girls to grab the picnic lunch.

G.B. took off his summer suit coat, loosened his tie, and rolled up his shirt sleeves. His car blew dust in his face as it moved toward civilization.

"G.B., this is going too far!"

He glared at her. "Move the baskets of tomatoes closer to the road, and Dixie, you and your sister take off those fancy shoes."

The girls obliged and dug their bare feet into the river-bottom sand.

It wasn't long before a white car pulled up to the little stand. "Howdy, neighbor," G.B. crooned, as he opened the man's car door for him. "We got the finest tomatoes in the bayou. How many for you?"

The stranger said, "Give me six or seven."

"Here's some red peppers, on the house, to go with them. Got nice watermelons too, not Texas melons, but grown not more than a stone's throw from this stand."

The white car drove away well supplied with homegrown garden goodness and G.B. counted the cash.

Lizzie unpacked their picnic lunch and G.B. ate with a big appetite. He added some tomatoes to their fare. The flies swarmed and the sun pointed down on G.B.'s head. He mopped his sweat and sang to himself.

The cars came and went. G.B. sold like a man undertaking a new vocation. An hour disappeared and the black Mercedes, bearing a smiling fruit-stand owner, returned. G.B. and the man grinned after the money changed hands—heaps of change and folded bills. G.B. climbed back into his car and left the man and his stand and the dust alone again. They traveled south.

Arkansas appeared. The sign on the side of the road denoted the end of Missouri and a new beginning . . . the state of Arkansas. A greener scene replaced dry and dusty.

"Lizzie, look over there. Is that fellow plowing with a team of mules? Like my daddy did . . . like Daddy." G.B. halted the car and crawled out. He stepped onto the uneven, freshly plowed soil. The girls and Lizzie trailed after, but settled under the shade of a massive pecan tree for protection from the relentless sun.

"Captain, seems to me you're still plowing the old-fashioned way. Don't you use a tractor for this work?"

The farmer looked at G.B. from the top of his sunburned head down to his snakeskin shoes. "Son, don't you know you should wear a hat in this heat?" Without a hitch in his rhythm, the farmer continued down the row. "Been doing it this way for forty years. Got about the best mules a man can have. Mighty nice shoes you're wearing. Aren't you afraid this powerful red dirt will cure them?"

G.B. said in a small voice, "My poppa used the mules. Guess with times changing, I'm just surprised. Don't mean any offense. I'm a country boy myself."

The stranger stared at G.B.'s shoes, spit some tobacco on the ground and called to his mules with a soft "git." The three of them moved down the row. G.B. turned toward his family who hailed him on, impatient to be gone.

G.B. walked to the pecan tree and sat down. "Lizzie, do I have another pair of shoes in the car?"

"Just your mud shoes in the trunk."

"Well, would you get those for me."

G.B. left his fancy shoes under the tree for the old man. He continued on his trip wearing shoes caked with Mississippi mud.

Memphis appeared. She stood in lights with hotels and parkways. G.B. signed his family into a Holiday Inn in time for dinner before the show. The movie turned out to be crowded. G.B. stood in front of the theater afterwards, a man with dust on his clothes and the residue of the hot sun on his head. They walked around in the city lights and finally drove to their hotel. G.B. removed his rumpled suit and walked to the pool to swim in the moonlight. A child of the Mississippi River, who never learned to swim, he jumped into the ten-foot expanse of night water and dog-paddled across the pool. He challenged the cool, glowing water until his feelings of fatigue insisted he go to his room and sleep in a bed away from home.

G.B. dreamed that night that he was a child again, the size of a yardstick, sick with the flu, but anxious for Christmas morning to begin. His mother was there. They didn't have a Christmas tree, but a fire burned in the oil stove. Morning brought him candy from Santa. G.B. looked at his mother's stained, callused hands. Someday, he thought, he was going to have enough money to buy real things. He awoke from his dream glad to know that those days of raggedy wanting were over. G.B. rolled over and touched Lizzie's arm. Her eyes opened.

"What is it, G.B.?"

"Do you think it's going to rain? Those beans could stand another shower, about an inch."

Lizzie put her arm across G.B.'s chest. "Sure, G.B., we'll get a good rain."

In the morning, Dixie and Ruth Ann walked arm-in-arm with G.B. to a small restaurant for a breakfast of country-cured ham, biscuits, and gravy.

The rain fell on G.B.'s dusty car as he finished his second cup of coffee. Laying a five-dollar tip on the table, he went out in the rain. His family followed. G.B. twirled around with his arms outstretched and his face turned upward. Dixie grasped his hands and they danced. G.B.'s change fell out of his pockets and onto the pavement. Their feet moved over the money as the rain poured down.

An old man stood in the doorway watching the hoopla. He yelled, "Hey, boss, what's going on?"

"This rain is worth more than a million dollars," G.B. announced. He stopped and stood still. With his country hands in his pockets, he thought of soybeans growing in even rows lapping up the precious rain.